melody
of love

HildaAnn Stahl

melody of love

HildaAnn Stahl

moody press
chicago

© 1975 by
THE MOODY BIBLE INSTITUTE
OF CHICAGO

ISBN: 0-8024-6509-9

Printed in the United States of America

Dedicated with love
to my parents,
JAY AND ZELMA CLEMENTS

Contents

1

The Accident

"I'M GOING. I'M GOING! I'm really going!" sang Melody Robins as she skipped and twirled across the pasture to find her mare. She jumped over a prairie dog hole, ran along a grassy knoll, and finally spotted the mare grazing near a grove of cottonwoods.

"Hi, Misty," called Melody, waving her arm high. "No baby yet?"

The mare lifted her head, whinnied then continued eating.

"Don't wait too long, Misty. I'm going to Mexico and I want to see your foal before I go." The magic word, Mexico, sent her twirling excitedly, her long blond hair flowing out behind her. Mexico in three more weeks!

Melody turned back toward the ranch, singing the song that her trio had sung the night before, the song that had won them the summer trip to Mexico. Two fabulous months in Mexico! Traveling from town to town singing songs that could help others to accept

Christ. What a perfectly wonderful, fabulous, spectacular way to spend the summer!

"Lord, help me to do my very best for You," she breathed as she stopped at the white board fence and looked around at her home. Even the ranch had a fresh look. The red and white barns and outbuildings looked brighter than usual. Melody looked at the horse barn just across the fence. She knew her sister, Betty, was in there with her newborn filly. Melody saw Tim, one of the ranch hands, coming out of the dairy barn with a pitchfork over his shoulder. Chickens ran around in their pen near the chicken house. Neil, the cook, came out of the cook shack and flapped the large tablecloth until all the crumbs from the early morning breakfast were gone. From where Melody stood she could hear him whistling gaily. The bunkhouse was deserted because all the hands were out with Mr. Robins, haying. The foreman's house was deserted too because Charlie and Wade had gone to Buckton to Hank's high school graduation. Melody smiled as she rested her chin on her arms across the top of the fence. Wade would be so happy for her. She couldn't wait to tell him.

The dog's barking drew her attention from Wade, and she looked toward the doghouse that stood just to the side of the ranch house and garage. Melody tried to see what he was barking at but couldn't. "Good old Touser," she said, smiling. Even Touser, the dog that was part everything, looked great.

Melody exuberantly twirled around and shouted, "I'm really going!"

Just then Betty came out of the horse barn. "Melody,

come here. I want you to take another look at my filly."

Melody climbed over the fence and ran to the barn. "What's she doing now?"

"Having a late breakfast," said Betty, her brown eyes sparkling. "Come look. That little gal is the greatest!"

"I remember feeling the same way about Misty when I was twelve," said Melody, smiling. "She was my first foal to train by myself. Now, she's going to have a foal."

The girls walked into the barn. Melody had to wait a minute before her eyes adjusted to the dimness.

Betty opened the stall door and stepped in. Melody followed and Betty closed the bottom half of the door.

"Show us your baby, Rina," said Betty softly.

The mare turned to look at the girls, then nudged the filly around as if to show her off.

"Isn't she perfect?" asked Betty with a long sigh. "And I get to train her by myself. I'll have so much fun."

"Have you decided on a name yet?" Melody leaned against the stall door.

"Not yet. But I'll think of one." Betty turned to Melody. "Did you find Misty?"

"Yes. Still not ready to foal. I hope she does before I go to Mexico."

"Mexico! Just think, my sister is going to Mexico. But I knew you'd win. Your trio was naturally the best."

"Thanks, Betty."

"It must be great to be seventeen and get to do so much. I can hardly wait until I'm thirteen. Just seventy-three days."

"You have it down to the day, don't you?" asked Melody with a laugh. "I know how you feel. Being a teen-ager is usually great. Especially now. I can't believe I'm really going to Mexico in just three weeks."

"How could it be any other way, Melody? Your trio was the best. I could have told you that a long time ago." Betty flipped her hair back with her small brown hand.

"Oh, Betty," said Melody, laughing and tugging play-fully at Betty's hair. "I guess I'd better go in. Mom will be going to town in a few minutes and I want to see her before she goes." Melody dashed toward the house as her mother walked toward the car parked in front of the garage.

"Wait, Mom!"

Mrs. Robins stood by the car and watched Melody dash to her.

"How long do you think you'll be in town, Mom?"

"About three hours, I guess. I want to get groceries too."

"And the material for our trio's dresses."

"Yes. You wanted yellow flowered," said Mrs. Robins, taking her sunglasses out of her purse and putting them on.

"Yes."

"Did you find Misty?"

"She was back by the cottonwoods," said Melody, pointing in the general direction.

"Did she look all right?"

"Yes. I'm sure she'll foal before I go to Mexico."

"Mexico!" said Mrs. Robins, hugging Melody. "I think I'm as happy for you as if I were going myself. It'll be a great experience for you. And a rewarding way to witness for Jesus." She opened the car door and slid under the steering wheel. "Take care of everything while I'm gone. You and Betty get the work done that I told you about and fix dinner for Betty and Dad."

"I will, Mom. If you can't get yellow flowered material, get orange flowered."

"OK."

"If you can't get either, I don't know what to tell you."

"Lucy and I have talked it over. I'll come up with something beautiful." She started the car, slammed the door shut. "See you later, Melody."

Melody watched her mother drive out the circle drive, through the ranch gate and out onto the road. With her hands clasped together, she dreamily pictured how the trio would look in the dresses. They'd decided that the girls would dress alike and Aunt Lucy would wear something that would accent their dresses. Aunt Lucy was going as coordinator and piano player. Uncle Ben was the evangelist and driver. What a fabulous summer they'd all have!

"Hey, I have work to do," said Melody, dashing toward the barn. "Betty! Come on. We have housework."

Betty poked her head out of the barn. "Do we have to?"

"Yes."

"I want to stay here," Betty said with a pout.

"You can come back out as soon as the work inside is done."

Just then a pickup drove in the circle drive and around to the foreman's house.

"Charlie's home," shouted Betty, waving and running toward the battered old pickup. "Hey, Charlie! Guess what?"

Melody ran along with Betty. Wait until Charlie and Wade heard that her trio had won the trip to Mexico!

"What's up, girls?" asked the tall, weather-beaten cowboy. "It's not every day a guy gets mobbed by two pretty girls."

"Rina had her filly," said Betty, grabbing Charlie's arm and tugging him toward the horse barn.

"And our trio won the trip to Mexico," exclaimed Melody, hanging on Charlie's other arm. "Where's Wade?"

"He stayed in Buckton," answered Charlie with a grin that made his narrow face almost handsome. He looked from one excited girl to the other. "Looks like I can't be gone at all without everything under the sun happening."

"She's the most beautiful filly this ranch has ever had," exclaimed Betty.

"I heard that same thing a few years back when Melody's filly was born," said Charlie with a chuckle.

"We're leaving in three weeks for Mexico," said Melody as they entered the barn.

"That's my little singer," said Charlie, hugging Melody. "Wade will be mighty proud of you."

"There she is," said Betty, opening the stall door.

The mare turned to look at them then continued munching her hay. The filly butted around the mare's leg until she found what she was looking for. Spreading her legs out, her neck down, head up under the mare, the filly suckled, completely unconcerned about her visitors.

"She's mighty pretty alright," said Charlie, standing with his thumbs stuck in the back pockets of his jeans. "The naming of her is going to be some fun for you, Betty."

"I'll think of something. I wrote down Lili Borina and Rafkei. By putting them together I'll come up with a great name."

"When's Wade coming home, Charlie?" asked Melody excitedly.

"That son of mine wanted to spend a few days with his cousin Hank, and he should be back by the end of the week." He put his arm around Melody. "Wade's a lucky boy and I'm proud that you're his girl. Couldn't be a nicer one around."

"Not even me?" asked Betty, giggling mischievously.

"Well now, I hadn't thought about that," said Charlie, tugging Betty's hair.

"You know I'll be thirteen in just seventy-three days. After that it won't be long before I can date." Betty leaned against Charlie's arm, looked up at him and batted her eyelashes in an exaggerated fashion.

Melody laughed, making the filly jerk her head around to see them.

"I bet no one will be able to resist you, little lady," said Charlie, squeezing Betty.

"If the boys don't notice me, I'll beat 'em up," said Betty, tossing her head.

"Betty, you'll do no such thing!" exclaimed Melody.

"Oh?"

"Betty!"

"Guess not," she said, giggling.

"I guess not too," said Charlie, grinning.

Melody looked lovingly at Charlie. He was like a second father to them. She stood on tiptoe and kissed his weather-beaten cheek.

"You haven't done that in a long, long time," he said, hugging her. "I'm glad that you won the trip to Mexico. I'll miss you. But Wade? He'll be hard to live with while you're gone. We'll both miss you something awful."

"Me too," said Betty. "I'll have to do all the work then."

"Oh, you!" said Melody, pushing Betty playfully.

"I hate to break up this little party, girls, but I got a pickup of gear and groceries to unload," said Charlie. He sauntered out of the barn and across the yard to the pickup. To Melody's knowledge he never walked briskly.

"Into the house with us," said Melody, sighing. "I guess I'd rather stay out here too, but I promised Mom we'd finish the housework before she gets back."

"Race you then," said Betty, dashing toward the house with Melody on her heels.

Melody's heart exploded with love for everyone. She didn't even feel like fighting with Betty. At times her sister irritated her beyond endurance but not today and not ever again because life was terrific!

"I'll change the beds while you do the dusting," said Melody as they stopped in the kitchen for a glass of orange juice.

"Okay," mumbled Betty, taking a long drink of juice.

She rubbed the back of her hand across her mouth and sighed deeply. "That hit the spot."

"I'll say," said Melody, setting the glass in the sink. "Whew! I'm certainly glad we have air conditioning. It would be too hot to work in here otherwise."

"I like you when you're nice to me," said Betty, grinning.

"I like you when you're nice to me too. I'm so happy. I don't think I'll ever fight again."

"Will you take your guitar with you to Mexico?" asked Betty as she gathered the dust cloth and furniture polish.

"Yes. Our songs will be arranged so that we can rely completely on my guitar just in case we run across a church without a piano."

"I don't think I'll ever learn to play as well as you."

"Sure you will, Betty. Just practice. Hey, I'd better get upstairs." Melody hurried upstairs to her parents' room. She stripped off the sheets and pillowcases, singing gaily as she worked. She took clean bedding out of the linen closet and made the bed. "I'll sing forever," she said as she fluffed up the pillows. She pulled the lavender bedspread into place as she thought of how glad she was that her parents had given her piano, guitar, and voice lessons. She smiled as she remembered the times when she'd been forced to practice.

Lovingly she picked up Dad's Bible. She was glad that her folks had taught her to love the Lord, to have a personal trust in Him. She put the Bible down and hurried out of the room, down the hall to her brother's room. Dave wouldn't be home from college for three more days but she cleaned the room and changed the bedding. Dave would be excited about her trip to Mexico. Dave was nineteen and studying to be a veterinarian. He'd always said that he could doctor the horses and cattle on the ranch as well as old Doc Mac-Bean. He'd teased Dad about doing it at cut-rate prices because, he'd said, after all you can't charge your own dad that terribly high vet fee.

Melody laughed then broke into another song that the trio always sang. She twirled around the room and out the door. She bypassed the guest room. To her knowledge they weren't having anyone in there until September when her grandparents were coming from Oklahoma. She smiled. In their home you never could tell when a guest was coming. It was an unwritten rule in their household to offer the guest room to anyone who needed a place to sleep. Their pastor had often sent visiting preachers or folks who were low on funds or couldn't find a place to stay out to them. The Robins family was known as a "soft touch" family. Melody laughed outright. She'd rather be that way than never do anything for anybody.

Melody changed the bedding in Betty's room, shaking her head at the messy place. When would that girl ever learn to clean her room properly? After all, she was going to be thirteen in seventy-three days. Melody laughed. Seventy-three days. She was getting as bad as Betty.

In her own room Melody dusted, vacuumed the floor, and straightened her drawers as well as changing her bedding. She dropped the dirty laundry down the laundry chute. "Hey, it's time to fix dinner," she said, glancing at her watch.

"I'm done with the dusting," called up Betty. "What next?"

"Clean the bathrooms," said Melody, running down the stairs. "I'll start dinner. Dad'll be coming in before long."

"What'll you fix? I'm hungrier than all the ranch hands put together."

They laughed together. "I guess I'll toss a salad, mash potatoes, heat up green beans, and broil steaks for us. We have apple pie too that Mom made before she left this morning."

"Let's eat now."

"Can't."

"I'll die, Melody."

"How about a cookie and a glass of milk before you clean the bathrooms? That should tide you over."

"Good enough," said Betty, dashing to the kitchen.

By the time Betty was finished with her snack and out of the kitchen Melody had the green beans boiling in one pan and the potatoes in another. From the refrigerator she took the lettuce, tomato, green pepper, onion, radishes, the last hunk of avocado and set them on the work table. By the time she had the salad tossed it was time to heat the oven and put the steaks to broil. When she slid the three large T-bone steaks into the broiler she was as hungry as Betty.

Melody heard the back door open and close and knew her dad was in from the hay field.

"Dinner smells good," he said, poking his head into the kitchen. He was a tall, slender, suntanned, good-natured man. "I'll wash up and be right down."

"OK, Dad."

Melody was mashing the potatoes when Betty dashed in.

"What shall I do, Melody? Eat?"

"Set the table first. You can't eat until it's on."

Betty stuck her finger in the potatoes then popped it into her mouth. "Good."

"Keep your finger out of the food. Are you a baby?"

Betty wrinkled her nose at Melody and then quickly set the table.

"Butter the beans, Betty," said Melody, taking the steak out and putting one delicious smelling piece of meat on each plate. She put on the dish of creamy mashed potatoes, then the bowls of salad. "You forgot the dressing, Betty. Get French and Thousand Island both."

"OK. Anything else?" she asked as she put the items on the table.

"Just Dad."

"I'm right here," he said, sitting down.

The girls dropped into their chairs, folding their hands in their laps.

"Looks so good I could eat all day," said Mr. Robins, grinning. "Betty, would you pray?"

"Sure." They bowed their heads and Betty said grace.

"Mom should be coming home soon," said Melody as she poured Thousand Island dressing on her salad.

"Don't count on it, girls. That mother of yours loves to shop. Let her loose in town alone and she'd stay the day and not notice." He sliced a hunk of steak and stuck it in his mouth. "Delicious, Melody. You know how to make your old dad mighty pleased."

"You're a good cook, Melody," said Betty.

"Thanks." Melody turned to her dad. "Are you look-ing forward to having Randy for the summer?"

"I sure am. He's quite a baby."

"I'm glad Aunt Lucy's leaving him with us," said Betty. "I'll like having a baby around."

They talked about Melody's trip to Mexico, Betty's filly, and Melody's mare.

After the apple pie Mr. Robins slid back his chair and stood up. "Back to work for me, girls."

"Don't work too hard, Dad," said Melody, smiling. It was a joke because she knew he worked harder than any of his men.

The phone rang as Mr. Robins walked past so he an-swered. After he listened for a while he fumbled for a chair and sank down.

Betty and Melody rushed to his side, waiting to hear the bad news.

Finally Mr. Robins hung up and leaned forward, groaning.

"Dad! What is it?" asked Melody sharply.

"Mom . . . your mom's been . . . been in a bad car accident. That was the hospital in Clearmount." He jumped up. "I've got to go to her. Melody, take care of things here for me. Tell Charlie."

"Can't we go along, Dad?" wailed Melody, clutching his shirt.

"Poor Mom," said Betty, sobbing.

Mr. Robins pulled himself together enough to com-fort them. "I need you to stay home to look after every-thing. I'll call as soon as I know anything. Pray, girls. Pray for Mom."

"We will, Daddy," said Melody, dabbing at her tears. "Hurry to Mom. Don't worry about us." Already she was sending up silent prayers for her mother.

2

Monster Matt

MELODY AWOKE but she didn't want to open her eyes and face the day. Why not? Wasn't it the same as yesterday? Wasn't she overjoyed about going to Mexico for two wonderful months?

Then a picture of Dad flashed across her mind. He was saying, "I'm sorry, honey, but because of Mom's accident you'll have to stay home. We can't afford to hire someone so you'll have to do her work." He'd said more but she only felt the dreadful words, "can't go."

Fresh tears slid down the sides of her face into her ears. She dabbed them away with the flowered sheet. No trip to Mexico! No trip. No trip.

She flipped onto her stomach and buried her head in her pillow, sobbing until her throat hurt and her head throbbed.

Several minutes later she listlessly climbed out of bed, dressed and walked downstairs to the kitchen.

She jerked open the cupboard door, pulled out a bowl and pancake mix, and stirred up a batch of batter.

She poured pancake batter on the hot griddle, heedless of the drips that ran down the side of the container and landed on her tennis shoe. Angry tears slid down her cheeks. How unfair life was! How very, very unfair!

"Good morning, Melody," greeted Betty cheerfully as she dashed into the kitchen.

Melody bit her tongue to keep from snapping at Betty. She flipped the pancakes fiercely. How could Betty sound so cheerful?

"Aren't you talking this morning?"

Melody glared at her.

"Are you the same girl, Melody? Only yesterday you were real nice to me."

"Yesterday Mom was OK and I was going to Mexico. Now, Mom's in the hospital and will be for two or three weeks and I can't go to Mexico!" Her throat tightened and she couldn't say another word without crying.

"It's bad for you but maybe you can go another time."

"I want to go this time," she said through clenched teeth, her eyes snapping. She wanted to strike out and hurt everyone like she was hurting.

"Don't get mad at me."

"Then leave me alone!" She turned back to the pancakes in alarm. "Now, look what you made me do! The pancakes are burned." Melody flipped the burned ones into the sink. Everything was going wrong! How was it that life was so smooth and beautiful for so long then all at once, everything was so terrible?

"Don't blame me for everything!" cried Betty, her hands on her hips.

Melody clenched her fists and glared at Betty. She wanted to slap her but she knew she didn't dare. "Set the table and stop bothering me." She turned back to her pancakes as Betty opened the cupboard door.

"Morning, girls," greeted Mr. Robins cheerfully as he entered. "I just called the hospital, and Mom had a very good night. She's really all right. Thank the Lord. I called Dave and told him." He sat down at the table. "Coffee smells good, Melody. Would you pour me a cup?"

Melody picked up the coffee pot and stomped across the floor. She poured the coffee, splashing some on the tablecloth, turned without an apology, and stomped back to the stove.

"Betty, get the syrup," snapped Melody. "Can't you do anything right? Do I have to tell you every move to make?"

"Melody," said Mr. Robins sternly.

"Don't bawl me out, Dad. Betty's the one who needs scolding. She's so dumb."

"Melody!" warned Mr. Robins. "I know it's hard on you to miss out on the trip to Mexico. It's a big disappointment, but it can't be helped. With Mom in the hospital we need you at home. You have every right to be upset, but don't take it out on your sister or anyone else. You are old enough to handle disappointment. Please, act your age."

Melody stood staring unseeingly out the window, her back stiff and straight, her mouth shut tight.

"Look at me, honey," continued Mr. Robins.

Slowly Melody turned around but she wouldn't meet his gaze.

"You're young yet, Melody. You'll have another chance to go to Mexico." He took her hand and held it gently. "I am so sorry that you can't go. I know what it means to you and I know how disappointed you are. Try to be happy. We'll see that you get a trip to Mexico maybe after you graduate."

Melody jerked her hand away. "I don't want to go to Mexico. I don't want to do anything. I'll stay home and work like a slave and die right here, a hard working miserable slave!"

"That will be enough of that kind of talk, young lady. Take this disappointment in your stride. Don't let it throw you. It can't be helped. Make the best of it."

"I won't," stormed Melody with her hands on her hips, her eyes blazing.

"You're a big baby," said Betty.

"Shut up."

"Make me."

"Girls!"

"Sorry, Daddy," mumbled Betty, sitting at the table.

Melody glared from one to the other then dashed out of the house, slamming the door with a sharp bang. She dashed across the yard, her blond hair blowing around her slender shoulders. Why, oh why did things happen that way? Why didn't God take care of everything the way she wanted it? Melody climbed the fence, jumped down, and raced across the grassy pasture until her lungs ached and a sharp pain jabbed her side. She dropped down in the tall grass and buried her face in her hands. "O God, don't You care about me? Don't You care?" Tears streamed down her face, wetting her hands. Her throat ached from crying so hard. She beat her fists against the ground. "Why? Why? Why?"

"Hey, why all the tears?"

"Wade! Oh, Wade!" Melody jumped up and flung herself at him.

"Poor Melody," he said gently as he held her. He let her cry a while longer then reached in his back pocket and pulled out his hanky. "Wipe those tears away, honey."

She lifted her tear-stained face and searched his eyes. She put her hand against his cheek. "Oh, Wade. I'm so miserable."

"I know." He wiped the tears off her face and gave her the hanky to blow her nose. "I came home when I heard about your mom and about you missing the trip. I want to help."

She blew her nose then stuffed the hanky in her jeans pocket. "Why did it happen, Wade? You've been a Christian as long as I have. Tell me what you think. Why would God allow Mom to be hurt and me to miss Mexico. Why?"

"I don't know, Melody, but I do know that the Bible says that all things work together for good to them that love God. That's a promise that you can cling to during this hard time."

"But I want to go to Mexico. I was going to work for the Lord."

"I know."

"Now what will I do?"

"You'll stay home and do something for the Lord here."

"The way I feel I won't be any good to anyone."

"Melody, you're just hurt now. I know you. You'll perk up and be your beautiful self again."

"I can't."

"I know you, Melody. You can do it. Remember when we were kids and Dad was going to take us to the rodeo but he couldn't the last minute?"

Melody smiled hesitantly. "I remember. I spent the first hour crying, the second hour listening to your plans for doing something fun anyway, and the rest of the day having a great time."

"We'll do that again, Melody. You cried, I talked, now let's both plan what we can do for the summer."

"Sure. Like what?" She choked back another tear. "What can take the place of a terrific trip to Mexico?"

"Who knows? We'll think of something." He brushed the hair from her face.

"It won't be the last time I cry about it but thanks for trying to help me this time."

"I love you. I had to help you." He pulled her close and kissed her. "I'll always be around when you need me."

"You're terrific, Wade," she said, looking up at him. She liked his red hair and brown eyes.

"I am proud of you for winning the trip, Melody."

"How was your cousin's graduation?" she asked, not wanting to think about her disappointment for fear she'd start crying again.

"Just great," he said. He put his arm around her shoulders and she put hers around his waist and they slowly walked toward the ranch. He stopped, looking down at her with a serious expression on his face. "I decided not to go to the state university."

"You did? Why?"

"Do you really want to hear?"

"Of course."

"I'm going to Bible school to become a minister of the Gospel."

"You're what?"

"I am."

"Honest, Wade?"

"Yes."

"When did you decide?"

"I've wanted to work for the Lord as a Christian businessman but now I feel the Lord called me to be a minister. I have a real burden for souls, Melody. I want to lead men and women, boys and girls to God. I want them to know the love, the peace, the satisfaction of serving Him."

"You sound like you could turn into quite a preacher."

"Are you making fun of me?"

"Oh, no. I think it's really great if that's what you want. I've thought a lot about serving God with music. That's why—why I was counting so much on going to Mexico. I felt I could really do something for God. But—but, now—"

"I know, Melody."

"Have you enrolled in the Bible school yet?"

"Yes. It might be too late but I gave it a chance anyway."

"They'd be dumb if they turned you down."

"Thanks."

"I mean it."

"I like you too. Look. There's Misty by the fence. She's about ready to foal, isn't she?"

"Yes. Have you seen Rina's filly? The one that Betty is going to train all by herself?"

"Not yet."

"Betty will never let you get by without seeing that filly. She's so excited about her that she'd sleep in the barn if we let her."

Wade chuckled as he put his arm around Melody again and they walked to the fence. "I remember when you were twelve and got your first one to train by yourself. I think I liked you even then although I pretended awfully hard to ignore you, especially when other boys were around playing with me. I didn't want anybody to think that you were special to me."

"I know. I did the same with you when my girl friends came over. The thing is they all got such crushes on you that you were usually the main topic of our conversations. If they didn't fall for you they did for Dave."

"When's Dave coming home?"

"At the end of the week. Maybe sooner because of Mom." Melody sighed loud and long. "I guess I'd better get back to the house. I have a lot of work to do. Work, work, work. That's my summer schedule now."

"Just lean on the Lord. He'll help you have a right attitude."

"OK, preacher."

"I'll try to remember not to practice my preaching on you."

"No, that's OK. How else will you learn? Besides, who else would listen?"

"Brat!"

"Preacher!"

Wade ruffled her hair.

"See you later, Wade," said Melody, climbing over the fence and running toward the house. She heard Betty call Wade, turned to look back at him, and saw him disappear into the horse barn with Betty.

Just as she reached the house she stopped in surprise as Dave drove around the circle drive and parked outside the garage. He jumped out of the car and hurried to Melody.

"How's Mom?" he asked in concern.

"Dad got a call from the hospital a while ago and they said she had a good night."

"What a relief! So, when can she come home?"

"Not for two or three weeks."

"Sorry about your trip, Melody."

"Me too."

"Hey, I forgot. I brought someone home with me for the summer."

"For the summer? But, Dave, how can we?"

"It's too late now. I planned on calling but didn't. He's already here and has nowhere else to go." Dave motioned for the young man to get out of the car. When he was beside Dave, Dave introduced him. "Matthew Chamberlain, Melody Robins. Matt is a missionary kid. His folks are in Peru."

"Hi, Matt," said Melody with a small smile. She studied his tall blond good looks. He would have been extremely handsome if it hadn't been for his bored expression and the sullen look around his mouth. He was definitely over-dressed for the country. Melody felt like a hobo in her worn jeans and sweatshirt.

Matt looked away from her to the ranch buildings and the wide open spaces surrounding them. "I don't know if I can take this country living. What do you do here for fun? It's so far away from the city."

"You'll get used to it," said Melody stiffly.

"Not if I can help it," he said coldly.

"Let's go see Dad. Is he still in the house?" asked Dave.

"I think so. Did you eat breakfast yet?"

"No. I'm as hungry as all the ranch hands put together."

Melody and Dave laughed together.

"What's the joke?" asked Matt peevishly.

"Dad always says that," explained Dave.

"That's funny?" asked Matt with a sneer.

"Of course it is," snapped Melody, glaring at Matt.

"Let's take a load of luggage in," said Dave, reaching into the backseat for a suitcase.

Melody hurried into the house. She didn't think she liked Matthew Chamberlain at all. How in the world could she put up with him for the summer?

Mr. Robins was sitting at the kitchen table with a cup of coffee when Melody entered.

"Feeling better?" asked Mr. Robins, standing up and putting his arm around Melody.

"I'll be OK, Dad. I'm sorry about my blowup." She

pulled away from him. "Dave's home and he brought a visitor for the summer."

"Hi, Dad," greeted Dave, rushing into the kitchen. He hugged his dad then stepped back. "Dad, meet Matt Chamberlain."

Melody busied herself with the pancakes while Dad, Dave, and Matt talked.

"Pancakes are ready," announced Melody, setting the steaming plate of buttermilk pancakes on the table.

"Pancakes? Don't you have anything lighter?" asked Matt, sitting at the table. "I'll have a soft boiled egg, glass of orange juice, and one piece of toast, lightly browned."

"What?" asked Melody incredulously. "You've got to be kidding."

"Why should I tease about that?" he asked coldly.

"Matt, I know you don't know our rules," said Mr. Robins, placing his hand lightly on Matt's shoulder. "But around here you eat what's fixed. If you want anything different you make it yourself."

"Me? I wouldn't do that! What kind of home is this, Dave?"

"My home and I love it," answered Dave stiffly. "You will too if you let yourself."

"Maybe I shouldn't have come."

"Matt, you had no other choice," said Dave softly.

"I'm not hungry," growled Matt, shoving his chair back and dashing from the house with a loud bang.

"Better fill me in about that boy," said Mr. Robins, sitting down.

Dave forked a pancake onto his plate, smeared it with butter and covered it with maple syrup. "Matt isn't the easiest guy to get along with. I know that. But he didn't have anywhere to go for the summer."

Melody helped herself to a pancake as she listened to Dave.

"His parents are missionaries in Peru. He was to stay the summer with a family in Lowell but they had him during Christmas vacation and then again during spring vacation. They said they absolutely wouldn't have him for the summer. He couldn't go to Peru and he had nowhere to stay so I told him if his parents agreed he could come here. I explained that he would be pulling his share of the work. Do you mind, Dad?"

"If we can help the boy I don't mind at all. It'll be more work for Melody but I'll assign chores for Matt that will help in the house too. Work should do him some good."

"I doubt if anything would help him," said Melody.

"What's his problem, Dave?" asked Mr. Robins, sitting forward and propping his elbows on the table.

"I don't know, Dad. He doesn't confide in anyone that I know of."

Suddenly the dog barked, someone screamed, and sundry noises split the air.

"What was that?" asked Mr. Robins, jumping up so fast his chair tipped over.

Melody and Dave ran with their dad to the source of trouble. It was in the horse barn.

"What happened, Betty?" asked Mr. Robins.

"That—that, whoever he is—" sputtered Betty, pushing her hair out of her face. Blood dripped from a scratch on her cheek.

"I didn't know anything would happen," said Matt belligerently. "All I did was tease the horse and baby."

"Matt, you aren't used to being around horses," said Mr. Robins firmly. "But Betty and the others are. If they tell you not to do something, then don't do it. We don't allow our animals to be teased for any reason. Especially not just to amuse a guest. Please, stay out of the barns and away from the animals until Dave can show you the ropes."

"Dave has ropes to show me? I couldn't care less." Matt strode out of the barn, his blond head in the air.

"Let me have a look at you, baby," said Mr. Robins, taking Betty's face in his hands. "It isn't as bad as it looks. Go clean it up and it'll be OK."

"Let me take care of my filly first," begged Betty, her brown eyes wide and sparkling from unshed tears. "That—that monster hurt her."

"His name is Matt," said Dave.

"I hate him," said Betty. "I'll hate him forever."

"Betty! Shame on you," said Mr. Robins, frowning. "You know better than to talk like that."

"He is terrible," whispered Melody, close to Betty's ear. "And he's staying for the summer."

"Oh, no!" wailed Betty.

"What's the matter now?" asked Mr. Robins from inside the stall where he was quieting Rina and the filly.

"Nothing, Dad," said Melody with a sheepish grin.

"Everything's OK now," said Dave as he and Mr. Robins stepped out of the stall. "Now, we'll fix up our baby."

"Me you mean?" asked Betty, making a face.

"Of course," said Dave, putting his arm around her thin shoulders. "Who else?"

They walked to the house. Matt was sitting on the back step with a sullen look on his face.

"Everything's fine, Matt," said Dave as Betty walked around Matt and into the house. "Come on. I'll show you your room and you can get unpacked."

Matt tossed his jacket onto a chair. "The coat closet is around the corner," said Dave.

"Let Melody hang it up," Matt retorted.

"Melody is busy," said Mr. Robins. "Around here, Matt, each one of us works."

"You can count me out," snapped Matt.

"Matt, I am the boss in this outfit, and I will be obeyed," barked Mr. Robins. "Take care of your clothes and meet me in the study as soon as possible."

Melody hadn't heard Dad speak that way in a long, long time. Everyone knew that he was the boss and he was never crossed. But, wow, Matt was really in for it. Melody hid a smile behind her hand. Good for Dad. Matt needed a firm hand. Or maybe a hard fist in the mouth.

Dave and Matt disappeared inside while Mr. Robins and Melody stood on the porch.

"I'm going to see Mom as soon as the meeting in my study is over," he said. "I'll be back by suppertime I think."

"OK, Daddy. Tell Mom I miss her. Tell her—tell her that I'm going to be just fine about not going to . . . to Mexico."

"I'll tell her, honey. And I'll tell you I'm mighty proud of my singer." He hugged her quickly then hurried into the house to the study.

Melody went to the kitchen. She scraped the dishes and loaded them in the dishwasher. She was wiping off the table when Betty bounced in.

"I guess I'm going to live," said Betty with a grin. "Where's the monster Matt?"

"Probably in the study getting 'orders' from Dad," said Melody, laughing.

"I'd like to hear that."

"Me too."

"Shall we?"

"And get into trouble with Dad when he's in the 'I'm boss around here' mood?"

"On second thought I guess I'll go make the beds while you clean up in here."

"Betty."

"What?"

"Make Matt's bed extra careful."

"Why?"

"You know. The special way Dave showed us."

"You mean—"

"Yes."

"I'll be glad to, Melody." Betty giggled as she dashed away.

Melody wiped off the syrup pitcher, chuckling to herself.

3

Good-bye, Melody

MELODY LOOKED at the calendar on the kitchen wall as she polished the refrigerator. Only one more day before the trio would leave for Mexico. And just a short time before Mom would be released from the hospital. What a long three weeks!

Tears stung Melody's eyelids as she thought of the girl, Beverly, who was taking her place in the trio. She wasn't as good as Melody but she could carry the part well and she played guitar beautifully. Melody had to admit she was jealous that the trio had found a replacement so quickly. The girls did sing beautifully even without her.

"Loafing again?" asked Matt, coming up behind Melody and tugging the long blond braid that hung down her back.

"I'm not but it looks like you are," snapped Melody, stepping away from him. "I heard Dad tell you to clean the manure out of the barns. Three weeks you've been here. Three weeks of trouble."

"Now, Melody. It hasn't been that bad."

38

"Not all the time. You can be nice when you try."
She smiled in spite of herself. Sometimes she really did
like Matt. Then other times— "If you know what's
good for you, you'd better head for the barn."

"Do I look the type to clean barns?"

"There's no 'type' that does it. You were given the
job so you'd better get at it. Or do you want another
session in the study? You've had at least three already.
It looks like you'd learn."

"I can handle your old man."

"Matt! Don't talk about Dad that way!"

"Daddy's baby."

"Get out of here and do your work."

"Make me."

Melody stood with her hands on her hips, her eyes
snapping. "Matt, are you sure that you're nineteen
years old? You act younger than Betty. Some guys are
married at your age."

"You marry me."

"Are you kidding! When I'm old enough to get married I want a man. Not a baby."

"And Wade's that man?"

"Maybe. We aren't old enough to talk marriage yet.
He must finish college." Melody rubbed the refrigerator till it shone. "Why don't you grow up, Matt?"

"Grow up! Me? The Robins children are the ones
that need to grow up. You all practically bow down to
your dad. And the time you spent in the hospital with
your mother! This is free America. You don't have to
be a slave."

"What's wrong with you, Matt? You have a rotten
attitude toward life. You don't act like any missionary

kid I've ever seen. You are rude and mean and arrogant."

"But good looking."

"And lazy."

"Sounds like you really do love me."

"Love!" she cried, not hearing his sarcasm. "Why else would you be saying all these good things to me?"

"Matt, no one but the Lord could ever love you the way you act."

"Shut up, Melody Robins."

"Did I hit a sore spot?"

"I said shut up!" Matt glared at Melody until she dropped her eyes. "I don't want the Lord or anyone else to love me."

"Go do your work so I can finish mine."

"I hate cleaning out barns."

"When I'm done in here I'll come help you."

Matt stared in surprise then turned and walked out.

Melody rubbed the refrigerator vigorously. What had ever made her offer to help Matt? Was she losing her mind?

"I just saw monster Matt in here," said Betty, poking her head around the doorway. "Is he gone? I don't like to be around him any more than necessary. He still hasn't forgotten about my short sheeting his bed when he first came. It was so funny the way he yelled and ran out of his room ranting and raving. When he found out that I'd done it he vowed to get even. I told him he was even already because of the scratch on my cheek." Betty chuckled. "I don't think he's used to being teased, do you?"

"I don't think he's used to anything. You can't imagine what I just told him I'd do."

"What?"

"I told him I'd help him clean the barns."

"Let me feel your forehead. No, you don't have a fever. What in the world made you do a thing like that?"

"Stupidity. Or maybe this hot weather got to me."

"What is that terrible racket outdoors?" asked Betty, rushing to the window.

"It's Touser," said Melody, peering over Betty's shoulder. "Oh, no! Matt again. Look what he did to our poor dog."

"Come on," shouted Betty, dashing out the door with Melody close behind.

"Quiet, Touser," ordered Melody as she worked on his chain to release it enough to allow the dog to get off the doghouse. "Dad's going to hear about this. How could Matt think that putting the dog upside down on his house and then chaining him so he can't move is funny? Something is really wrong with him."

"I know. He needs a new head."

"I think a new heart," said Melody softly. Dear Lord, help me to lead Matt to Thee, she prayed silently.

"What?"

"Nothing, Betty. Down, Touser. You're OK now. Easy, boy. I'll get you some cold water."

"Monster Matt," mumbled Betty, turning and slowly walking back to the house.

Melody took the dog's water dish and filled it with cold water from the hose beside the house and carried it back to him. Touser barked sharply then lapped the water. Melody patted his head. "Good boy. Nice Touser."

Melody walked slowly back to the house thinking of a way she could help Matt. She changed into her barn clothes and went to join Matt in the horsebarn.

Matt was sitting on a bale of hay, a long straw sticking out of the corner of his mouth, and a pitchfork, its tines in the air, in one hand. "Do I look like one?"

"One what?"

"A farmer, of course."

"You couldn't look like a farmer if you tried. You look like what you are. A greenhorn. You act like a greenhorn and that wasn't one bit funny the way you tied Touser to the doghouse."

"How do you know it was me?" asked Matt, spitting the straw out.

"Who else would it be?"

"Maybe Wade."

"Not Wade. Wade is terrific. Besides he's not dumb enough to do that."

"I know. I know. He's your boyfriend and naturally you wouldn't think wrong of him."

"That's because there's nothing to think. Wade is terrific."

"So you said."

Melody looked around the barn. It was still as dirty as it had been. "I guess you've been waiting on me. You start on that end and I'll start on this end."

"Do you think you can do more than I can? I might be a city dude but I'm a lot stronger than a mere country girl."

"You are?"

"Don't get smart."

Melody walked to the center of the barn. "Here's the middle. Whoever gets here first, and remember, that's doing a good job, will be declared the best barn cleaner. And possibly the strongest."

"I'm ready," said Matt from his end.

"Get on your mark, get set. Go!" shouted Melody, hiding the smile as she watched Matt work with a frenzy. She'd give him a run for his money. He was going to know he'd had a contest when they were finished. Working at top speed she was almost done with her share when Matt triumphantly declared he was the winner.

"What'd I say?" he asked smugly, leaning against the nearest stall.

"You've won only if your side passes inspection," said Melody, walking along the barn aisle and into the stalls. "Matt! I am amazed! You did a better job than I ever do. You cleaned as good as Dad or Dave."

"Or Wade?"

"Yes. You did a terrific job."

"I'll finish your share if you want me to," he said, swaggering to where she'd left off.

"You can help me, then we'll do the dairy barn. Maybe I can beat you in there." Melody laughed, twinkling at Matt.

"You're nice when you try to be, Melody."

"You are too, Matt."

"Dave bragged so much about his family that I was prepared to hate all of you and do everything I could to make life miserable. I was wrong."

Melody smiled warmly, noticing how extra good looking he was when he smiled.

"Let's go have a glass of cold milk and a few cookies before we start the dairy barn," she said, standing her fork next to an empty stall.

"Sounds great," he said, standing his fork next to hers. "Let's go."

They walked to the house, talking and laughing.

They washed up, then Melody poured the milk and put a jar of gingersnaps on the table. Just as they finished eating Mr. Robins charged in.

"Young man, I've just been in the dairy barn and I see that you didn't get your work done. I thought we had come to an understanding."

"It's OK, Dad," cut in Melody. "He has the horse barn done, and he did a great job so I told him to come in for milk and cookies. He's going to the dairy barn now."

"You don't have to talk for me," said Matt stiffly. "I'll get at my job now."

"Sorry if I sounded gruff, Matt," said Mr. Robins, clamping his large hand on Matt's shoulder. "I know somewhere inside you is a decent, reliable young man. I want to see that young man."

"Do you think it's possible, Mr. Robins? I don't," growled Matt. He rushed out, slamming the door behind him.

"He is learning, Dad," said Melody, pouring a tall glass of lemonade and handing it to her father. "I think he needs a firm hand, but I also think he needs love from us."

"You're right, Melody," said Mr. Robins, sipping his

lemonade. "It's hard to believe that he is Dave's age. Have you noticed that he doesn't take part in church services? I think that boy needs our prayers too. I really do."

"Me too. How's Mom?"

"I called and she wants to come home right now. The doctor said not yet. He wants her there a while longer."

"I miss her, Dad. I hope she didn't mind that I didn't visit her today."

"She understands, honey. She and I are both proud of the way you took a hold here and worked like you enjoyed it."

"Not enjoyed but at least endured."

"I'll go check on Matt. I want to make sure that young man is busy," said Mr. Robins, setting down his glass.

"Remember, Dad. A word of praise does a lot more good than a stiff scolding."

"Yes, Miss Robins."

"Oh, Daddy. I didn't mean to sound like that."

He kissed her and hurried out.

Melody rinsed out the glasses, put the cookie jar away and was just ready to join Matt when a car drove in. She looked out. It was Aunt Lucy and the trio. Melody reluctantly walked out to them, her mouth dry, her heart icy.

"Hi, Aunt Lucy," greeted Melody, opening the car door for her. She looked in the back seat at Jan, Sue, and Beverly. Her heart stuck in her throat and it was hard to smile.

"I brought the girls to show you their new dresses," said Aunt Lucy as she climbed out. She reached in and took Randy out of his car seat. "Get out and show Melody, girls. I had each one of them wear one of the new dresses."

Melody tried to be excited with the girls as they modeled the dresses. She couldn't talk around the lump in her throat. She blinked hard to keep the tears from falling.

"Melody, the girls and I feel so bad about you not going," said Aunt Lucy, putting her hand on Melody's shoulder and looking kindly at her. "We are so sorry that you must miss all the joy and fun we'll have. But, honey, the Lord will reward you for helping your parents when they need you so badly."

Melody eased herself away from her aunt. How could they know how she felt? They all were going. She had to stay behind.

"We've been practicing for hours each day," said Sue.

"Bev does almost as good as you," said Jan.

"Thanks," said Bev, then they all laughed except Melody.

"I have the itinerary finished," said Aunt Lucy, shifting Randy from one hip to the other. "It'll be a perfect summer."

Melody opened her eyes wide and swallowed hard to force the tears back.

"Sue, take the keys and unlock the trunk so we can get Randy's things out. I'm so glad you're taking Randy for me, Melody," said Aunt Lucy, handing the baby to Melody.

"What?" asked Melody in surprise as she opened

Randy's hand and extracted a handful of her hair. How had they forgotten to discuss it with her?

"Didn't your mother tell you? She said she'd okay it with you about leaving Randy here like I'd planned."

"With me?"

"Is it all right? I mean, I've planned on it and all. I was sure Zelma would have told you our plans. I saw her just yesterday in the hospital and she said she'd remember to say something to you. If—if it's out of the question I could—could— No! There isn't anything else I could do. Oh, please, Melody. Won't you take care of Randy? I can't do anything else. I must go with the trio. If I can't go, they can't either. Please, Melody."

For just a minute Melody wanted to shout out that she couldn't care less if the trio or Aunt Lucy went to Mexico, but instead she agreed to take Randy.

"I've written down his schedule. If you don't follow it, don't worry. He's nine months old and it won't hurt him to be off. Thanks, Melody. You're super." Aunt Lucy hugged her, Randy and all.

Melody looked down at the baby's bald head and wondered how she'd ever thought he was cute. She'd baby-sat with him hundreds of times since he was born and he'd seemed so adorable. But, now, she thought he looked downright ugly.

Baby-sitting instead of going to Mexico to sing! What could be worse?

4

Tedium

MELODY WEARILY STUFFED the last load of sheets into the washer, added the detergent and closed the lid as Betty danced into the room.

"What's my job today, Melody?" she asked cheerfully, leaning her elbows on the dryer, chin in hand. "I feel like I could fight a wildcat."

Melody pushed her hair out of her face, tired already. "You can take care of Randy."

"Are you kidding? Watching that baby is like herding six wildcats. He can find more trouble to get in." She sighed loud and long. "I thought I was so smart teaching him to walk so Aunt Lucy and Uncle Ben would have a big surprise when they got home."

"Even when he only crawled he got into plenty of trouble. It would be easier if he was just tiny and stayed in bed all day."

"Have you been in to see Mom yet this morning?" asked Betty as they walked out of the laundry room.

"I haven't had a chance."

"It's so good to have her home."

"I'll say. Even though it means waiting on her," said Melody. "Putting a bed in the sewing room so she could be downstairs sure helps me."

They stopped outside their mother's door and looked in.

"Good morning, girls," she said, smiling. "Come in and talk to me."

"Only for a minute," said Melody, sitting on a chair by the bed. "Randy will be waking up soon. If I'm not right there to take him out of the crib, he tries to climb out."

Mrs. Robins smiled. "I remember when you children did that. It's nice having a baby in your crib. But it does make me feel old knowing that my baby is twelve."

"Almost thirteen, Mom. Just next month," said Betty proudly.

"But she still doesn't keep her room clean," said Melody.

"What did I tell you, Betty? You are to keep it clean by yourself. I can't help you now and Melody is too busy." She turned to Melody. "How is everything working out?"

"Not too bad. Only—only I don't have time for myself anymore. With Randy around I don't have time to breathe properly."

"I know how you feel, honey. I think we can work something out." She frowned thoughtfully. "I have it," she said, clapping in delight.

"What, Mom?" asked Melody, smiling at her mother's enthusiasm.

"I'll make up a schedule. Everyone will have a turn watching Randy. Even Dave can help."

"And Matt?" asked Betty with a giggle.

"Of course Matt," said Mrs. Robins, reaching for her clipboard and pen. "Girls, come back later and I'll have it down pat."

"Okay, Mom," said Betty.

"See you later," said Melody, walking toward the door.

"Wait, Melody," said Mrs. Robins. "Has Misty dropped her foal yet?"

"Not yet and I'm beginning to worry."

"Is she all right otherwise?"

"Yes. Dad says so, and so does Charlie."

"Honey, come here a minute," said Mrs. Robins, patting the edge of the bed. "Now that Betty is out, I want to ask you how things are between you and Wade. I've been hearing a little that makes me think that love isn't running as smoothly as it once did."

Melody sank down on the bed. "Oh, Mom. It's just that I never have time for Wade. It's been a month since we've had a real date. We go to church together but I always have Randy and sometimes Betty, Dave, and Matt. Wade gets upset because I have more time for Matt than for him. But, Mom, it's just that Matt's around the house and Wade is always out on the range working. But—but Wade thinks that I'm trying to break up with him and taking the easy way out with my work routine."

"I'm sorry, honey."

"Mom, Wade can't think I like Matt. He knows I'm

his steady. I wouldn't even consider dating anyone else."

"Does Matt know that?"

"Of course. At least I think so. Besides Matt doesn't like me any better than I like him."

"You'll work it out, Melody." Mrs. Robins patted her hand and smiled lovingly. "You're learning more than you know this summer. It's different than you'd planned but you're learning many valuable lessons."

"Am I?" she asked, barely concealing her anger.

"Just trust, Melody. God knows what He is doing with your life."

Melody mumbled something then left before she exposed her true feelings. What had she learned so far? To hide her true feelings? To keep working even though she wanted to quit?

Randy's demanding wail sent Melody dashing upstairs to her room.

"Morning, Randy, doll," she said, tickling him until he gurgled with laughter. "Come to Melody." She held her hands out and Randy put his in hers. "You're not really too bad, Randy. It's just that you take up so much time."

Randy laughed and kissed her wetly.

Melody changed his diaper then carried him downstairs to the kitchen for breakfast.

Matt was sitting at the table with a glass of milk and a piece of toast. "Hi. How's the kid?"

Melody looked at Matt in surprise. Since he was being polite, she would be too.

"He just woke up and he's really hungry," answered

Melody, putting the baby in the highchair and tying his bib in place.

"Here, Randy. Have some toast," said Matt, handing the baby a crust of his toast.

"He can't eat that!"

"Of course he can. See? He loves it. Good, isn't it, fellow?"

"He's eating it."

"Sure. It'll keep him happy while you fix his egg. Want me to feed him?"

"You?"

"Me."

"But—but, Matt—"

"I've fed more babies in my time than you. I can do it without a mess or bother. Watch."

Melody watched as Matt quickly scrambled an egg. He put the egg on a plate, added applesauce, and poured a half glass of milk.

"Nothing to this," he said, sitting down and pulling the highchair close. "Bite, Randy? Good eggs. Open wide." He held the spoon out and Randy opened his mouth and Matt shoved it in. "Easy as that."

"I can't believe it."

Randy cooed and opened his mouth for more.

"Why won't he eat like that for me?"

"Magic touch, I guess."

"I guess so too. Matt, you have yourself a job from now on."

"I'll take him out to play when he's done eating."

"Honest?" This was a side of Matt that she hadn't seen before.

"Why so surprised? I am able to do some things."

"But—but, take care of Randy! I'm flabbergasted, surprised, but absolutely delighted. Randy takes up so much time. Do you know I haven't touched my guitar for so long my fingers probably won't know what to do."

"I didn't know you played guitar."

"That's how long it's been." Melody grinned. "I can play pretty good if I do say so myself."

"I can too. I took lessons in Peru from a man that could play guitar like you wouldn't believe."

"I'd love to hear you, Matt. Why didn't you say something before this?"

"I don't have my guitar. I left it at school because I didn't think I'd have any use for it."

"You can play mine."

Matt gave Randy the last bite of egg and applesauce then held the glass so he could drink his milk. Matt looked up at Melody with a delighted smile. "We'll put on a show for Randy. Babies love guitar music."

"What else do you know about babies, Matt?"

"You name it, I know it. There were twins the last place I stayed."

"Bath?"

"Yup."

"Dress?"

"Yup."

Melody hugged Matt excitedly. "Oh, Matt! You are a lifesaver. You really are. If you take Randy now, I can go to the barn to check on Misty."

"I was there before I came in. Still nothing."

"Wow! I'm going crazy waiting on her."

"Hear that, Randy? Let's get away from this crazy

girl." Matt laughed as he wiped off Randy's hands and face.

"I laid out his clothes on my bed."

"OK," said Matt, lifting Randy out of the highchair. "Just leave little Randy baby to old Matt."

"With pleasure."

Melody rushed through the rest of the work. Matt was romping on the lawn with Randy when she ran to the horsebarn.

She stepped inside the barn and stopped a minute to enjoy the smell of horses and listen to the sounds of an occasional stomping of hooves and a soft neigh.

"Morning, Melody." Wade was leaning against the half open door of Misty's stall.

"Hi, Wade," she said, looking up at him with a smile. It was so good to be alone with him even for a minute.

He didn't smile back.

"Are . . . are you mad at me, Wade?" Her heart skipped a beat.

"I don't know! All I know is that I never get to see you or be with you more than a minute of the time without some interruption." He ran his fingers through his red hair.

"I know," she said, resting her forehead against his arm. She stood that way for a minute then stepped closer to the stall and looked in. "How's Misty?"

"Still nothing."

"I don't know who feels worse about it. Me or my mare. Poor thing can hardly get around. It can't be much longer, can it, Wade?"

"No. No way."

Melody brushed a piece of straw off Wade's shoulder. "Tell me how your junior boys Sunday school class is."

"Just great," said Wade, beaming. "Two boys accepted Christ last week. And the attendance has increased at least fifty percent. They really love studying Paul's missionary journeys."

"The boys know you care about them," added Melody. "Our pastor hasn't had as much trouble with them during worship service since you took over the class."

"I told them right out they were sinning if they didn't reverence God's house."

Melody watched a fly buzz around Misty as she once again thought what a terrific Christian Wade was. He would make a wonderful minister. She looked up at him with a smile. "I'm proud of you, Wade."

"Thanks," he said, grinning, his brown eyes warm. They leaned against the stall door, silently watching Misty.

"Hey! Guess what?" She faced him with her hands clasped and her eyes shining.

"What?" he asked, grinning.

"Matt knows how to take care of Randy. He's watching him right now."

The smile froze on Wade's face. "So?"

"So, that's great!" Couldn't Wade understand anything? He had certainly changed since Matt had come. And not for the better. She felt her temper rising.

"What's so great about a thing like that?"

"If you don't know, I'm not telling you." She stomped her foot, her eyes snapping. "You can't stand to think that a city boy can do something better than you."

"You like him, don't you? You like him too much, Melody. You're my girl. Remember?"

"How can I forget when you put it that way?" she asked through clenched teeth.

"Any time you want to give me my class ring back just feel free. It is a free country and you're a free human being."

"Do you want it back? Is that why you're getting so upset? You want it back so you picked a dumb excuse like Matt to fight about so I'd give it back and you wouldn't have to come right out and ask for it."

"You don't know me at all, do you, Melody? If you think I wouldn't have the nerve to ask for it back, then you don't know me. I'm not a coward."

"Did I say you were? I don't even know what this dumb argument is all about."

"It's your dumb argument, not mine."

"Do you want your ring back, Wade?" Her mouth was dry and she locked her fingers together.

"If you want to give it back. What's the use of going steady if I can't even date you once in a while? You never have time for me."

"Is that my fault, Wade? Is it? No! It's not. I'd rather be with you any day than working like I've been working for the past weeks. I'm only seventeen and I feel like an old woman."

"Do you mean it?"

"Mean what? That I feel rotten?"

"That you'd rather be with me."

"Of course I mean it."

"Oh, Melody. I'm sorry for getting so mad." He put

his arms around her and pulled her close. "I'd rather kiss you any day than fight with you."

"Me too," she said, lifting her face for his kiss. Her heart was light again.

"Melody! Come look at Randy," shouted Matt from the yard.

Melody pulled away from Wade and started for the door.

Wade caught her hand and pulled her back. "Tell him you've seen enough of Randy."

"Melody, come quick. He's hugging a kitten. Hurry," shouted Matt.

"Coming," called Melody, reluctantly pulling away from Wade.

"I might as well see this too," grumbled Wade, following Melody to the yard.

Randy was holding the kitten and rubbing his face against its soft fur, laughing in delight.

"That's what he wanted you to see?" grumbled Wade.

"Pretty kitty," said Melody, kneeling beside Randy and hugging him and the kitten.

"He's some baby," said Matt. He was sitting beside Randy, grinning proudly. "He loves that kitten. But he gets a little rough with it if you don't watch."

Melody sat down beside Randy with her arms around her knees. "Kitty, Randy. Kitty."

"Oh, brother!" said Wade.

"You have a problem?" asked Matt.

"Yeah. But not for long, I hope."

"You don't have to be so rude, Wade," snapped Melody.

"It seems to be what you like these days," growled Wade.

"If you don't like our company, you can leave," said Matt.

"Gonna make me?"

"If you want!"

"Wade! Matt! What in the world is wrong with you guys?"

"Take a walk with me, Melody," said Wade, holding his hand out to her.

"I guess I'm in the way," said Matt, jumping up and hurrying into the house, leaving Randy with Melody.

Melody carefully released the kitten, stood up, and picked up Randy. She glared at Wade. "What's wrong with you? You've made Matt angry. Now, who's going to watch Randy?"

"Want me to? Here, give him to me. If monster Matt can do it, so can I." But when Wade took the baby, he started crying in fright and wouldn't stop until Melody took him back.

"So much for that," she said coldly, turning and walking to the house with Randy in her arms.

5

Songs of Summer

"It's HERE! It's HERE! It's here!" shouted Betty, rushing into Melody's bedroom where she'd taken Randy to change his diaper.

"What is?" asked Melody excitedly as she scooped up Randy.

"Your foal. He's the most beautiful horse I've seen. Just great!"

"Let's go see him," exclaimed Melody, hurrying downstairs and then outside with Randy bouncing on her hip.

Misty's first foal. She couldn't believe after all the waiting that just like that he was finally here.

Melody rushed into the barn where Wade, Matt, and Dave were already looking over the top half of the door into the stall.

"He's perfect, Melody," said Dave with a grin. "You're going to have one great horse in a few years."

"Oh! Let me look!" she said as the boys stepped aside.

"I'll take Randy," said Matt, holding his arms out to

the baby. Randy squealed delightedly and leaned to-ward Matt.

"Thanks, Matt."

Wade pushed the door open and Melody stepped into the stall.

"Misty, what have you done?" she asked softly. "Did you give me a pretty little baby?"

The foal was still lying down, but at the sound of Melody's voice he flopped his long legs out in front of him and jerked up. He stood unsteadily on wobbly legs then darted forward, bumping into the side of the stall and falling down.

Misty nudged him with her nose.

"Try again, little fella," said Melody. Her heart was singing. She watched breathlessly as the foal stood up again and nudged his mother until he found his first meal.

Melody walked out of the stall, fastening the door behind her. "He was worth waiting for. Does Dad know?"

"Not yet," said Dave.

"I'll go tell him," said Betty.

"No. I will," said Melody, dashing out of the barn. Her blond hair whipped around her face. Her blue eyes sparkled.

"Daddy! Daddy!" she exclaimed as she burst into his study. "My foal's finally here. He is out of this world."

Mr. Robins pushed back his chair and stood up. "Great, honey. Let's go see him." He took his hat off the rack and followed Melody out.

"I wish Mom could see him."

"Good idea! Dave and I can make a chair with our arms and carry her to the barn."

"Oh, Daddy! That's terrific! I'll get Dave." She rushed to the barn, calling her brother. When he heard the plan he hurried to the house and went to Mrs. Robins' room.

"I'm really going outdoors," said Mrs. Robins, wiping tears from her eyes. "While I'm outside I want to see everything. Melody's new foal. Betty's. Even Touser and the kittens."

Tears stung Melody's eyes as she followed them out of the house. She'd been so busy feeling sorry for herself she hadn't taken time to realize how hard it was for Mom to be in bed for so long.

It seemed like a holiday as they walked around the ranch. Even Matt and Wade kept their animosity concealed. When they walked back to the house the phone was ringing.

"I'll get it," said Melody, dashing for the phone in the kitchen.

It was for her and it was a very strange call, a very surprising call. When she replaced the receiver she went to her mother's room.

"Mom, I just got the most unusual phone call. A Miss Jenkins from Mercy Hospital wants me to come in this afternoon to sing to the children in the pediatric ward."

"That's wonderful, Melody. I remember Miss Jenkins. I told her about your talent and your trip to Mexico. I also told her how disappointing it was for all of us that you couldn't go. I'm glad she called you."

"She said they'd booked Flanko the Clown but something happened and he can't make it. She didn't want the children disappointed. Oh, Mom! Do you think I can do it? I don't mean sing. I can sing but can I entertain children?"

"You know several children's songs, honey. I'm sure you can do it. If you want I'll write a program for you to follow."

"That's great, Mom!"

"How long? Did she tell you how much time you'll have?"

"An hour."

"I'll write down all the songs you know and make them into an order that will make the best presentation." Mrs. Robins' eyes sparkled with joy. Her cheeks were pink and she acted as if any minute she would bounce right out of bed.

"I'll take my guitar." Melody was breathless with excitement. "How about a story? I could tell them a story."

"Honey, I am so glad to see you happy again. I haven't seen you this bubbly since the day of my accident." Mrs. Robins wiped the tears out of her eyes and reached for the clipboard beside her bed.

"Oh, Mom! What about Randy?"

"Someone will take care of him. Betty can, I'm sure."

"What'll I wear? It should be something really bright. I know. My orange plaid dress." Melody kissed her mother's cheek and rushed out of the room and up to hers.

Melody took a quick shower, dressed, brushed her hair, picked up her guitar and hurried back to her mother's room.

"It's ready," said Mrs. Robins, holding out a piece

of paper. "I sent Betty after Dad and the boys so they could listen to you rehearse."

Melody read the program excitedly. "This is really great, Mom. It really is. Thanks loads."

As she tuned her guitar, Matt knocked and entered. "Thanks for inviting me to the family gathering, Mrs. Robins," he said, smiling warmly at her.

"You are part of our family, Matt."

Melody was surprised at the kind way he talked to her mother.

"How about letting me try out your guitar," said Matt.

"Sure," answered Melody, handing it to him.

Matt adjusted the strap, put it around him and over his shoulder.

As he played and sang, Melody and Mrs. Robins looked in pleased surprise at each other.

He can play, thought Melody. She watched him eagerly. He looked positively handsome with his blond hair and blue eyes and the happy look on his face.

"Matt! You are too terrific for words," said Melody when he finished. "Let's sing one together." She showed him the list. "What do you choose?"

Matt looked over the list then started strumming "Oh, Senior Del Gato." They sang together, their voices blending beautifully. Matt sang the lead and Melody sang the harmony.

Dave, Betty, and Mr. Robins came in during the song.

"You two should go into show business with that kind of singing," said Mr. Robins when they finished. "It sounded great."

"Why don't you work out the program to include Matt?" asked Mrs. Robins, smiling.

"How about it, Matt?" asked Melody excitedly as she put her hand on his arm and looked up at him.

"I'd love to," he answered in a low voice, looking only at Melody.

"How's Wade going to like that?" asked Betty, grinning and winking at Melody.

"Hush, Betty," commanded Mrs. Robins, frowning. "He won't mind at all, I'm sure."

Melody wasn't at all sure but she didn't have time to talk to him about it. If he wanted to get angry or jealous he'd have to.

She forgot about Wade as she and Matt sang together a few more of the songs. It was terrific to sing again, to hear the blending of her voice with another.

Later while Matt dressed, Melody took a few minutes of time to pray for their program. She wanted the gospel songs that they'd chosen to touch the hearts of the children.

"I'm ready," called Matt, knocking on her door.

"Me too," she said with a smile.

They walked to the car, Matt carrying the guitar.

"You drive," she said, handing him the keys.

"Won't your dad mind?"

"No." She knew her dad was beginning to trust Matt.

As Matt and Melody drove out of the circle drive Wade was driving in. Melody waved and watched him do a double take then glare angrily at her.

"Wade's temper goes good with his red hair," said

Matt, chuckling. "If he intends to be a preacher he'll have to learn to control it."

"Who told you he was going to be a preacher?" asked Melody sharply. She knew she hadn't and it wasn't something that Wade would confide to Matt.

"I heard him tell your dad and brother. They were very impressed. If you ask me, that's why he told them."

"You don't know Wade at all if you think that. He's a dedicated Christian."

"And a dedicated boy friend? Or does he go out with other girls when you aren't around?"

"Matt! Can't you talk about something else? Are you trying to upset me so you can do all the entertaining yourself?"

"Sorry. I'm jealous of Wade."

"Jealous!"

"He has everything. A girl, a nice father, good job, and he knows his future." Matt passed a slow-moving truck then continued. "I don't have even a family around. And I'll never have a girl like you."

"Of course you will. You'll find someone to love and someone to love you."

"I'll let that pass," he said, frowning. "I don't even know my future."

"How can that be? You've already finished one year of college."

"I'm only in college to help pass away time. I'd rather study than find a job. As long as I'm in school my parents pay the bills. When I'm out I'm on my own."

"You sound lazy."

"Do I? Maybe that's because I am. I haven't found anything I enjoy doing."

Melody twisted around in the seat so she could look at him. "You love taking care of Randy. In my opinion that's work with a capital W."

"I'm not built right to be a mother."

"But there are jobs connected with kids. Find one that will suit you."

He glanced at her thoughtfully then returned his attention to the road. "You really are good for me, Melody. It's too bad we don't fall in love."

"Oh, brother!" she said, twisting around right and looking out her window.

"Don't worry, I'm only teasing," he said, grinning.

"It's a good thing." She might know he couldn't get through one day without teasing her about something.

They rode the rest of the way in silence.

Miss Jenkins met them at the admittance desk. Melody introduced herself and Matt as they walked to the elevator.

"You'll never know how much this means to me as well as the children," said Miss Jenkins. "And to have two special services in one day will be extra exciting to the children. You can stay and perform after supper too?"

Melody smiled at the gray-haired nurse, admiring the fresh white uniform. "We'll love doing it."

"Right in here," said Miss Jenkins, pushing open the door to the sunroom.

Melody felt compassion flood over her at the sight of the kids. Some had arms or legs in casts, others were sitting listlessly in wheelchairs, while others were lying down.

"Children, Melody and Matt came to sing to you today," said Miss Jenkins, smiling at the children. "Melody, it's all yours."

Melody stood in front of the children with her guitar, trying not to feel nervous. "We're happy that we could come visit you today, boys and girls," she said as she played a few chords. "My first song is one that you might know. If you do, sing along with me." Melody sang the first verse of "Jig-a-long, Jig-a-long, Jig-a-long Home." The children laughed at first hesitantly, then forgot themselves and really laughed. At the beginning of the chorus one small boy joined in then stopped when no one else did.

Matt walked around the room singing the chorus with Melody and motioning for the children to join in. By the end of the chorus most of them were singing.

Melody sang verse after verse and the children with Matt joined loudly on each chorus. When the song ended, the applause was so loud Melody was afraid it would disrupt the hospital.

Matt took the guitar for the next song.

"You'll enjoy this funny little song," said Melody, smiling at the children.

They sang "Oh, Senior Del Gato" while Matt played extraordinarily well. The children clapped until Melody knew their hands stung.

The next song Matt sang alone.

Melody watched as he came alive, more alive than she'd ever seen him. His blue eyes twinkled with pleasure, his cheeks were flushed, and he was singing with his whole being.

Melody clapped as loud as the children when he finished.

He bowed and handed the guitar over to Melody.

She strummed as she talked. "Boys and girls, we've been singing fun songs that you've heard lots of times before, but now I want to sing a song that's not only pretty but has something special for you." She sang "Happiness Is the Lord."

"Sometimes we think we have nothing to be happy about. If your legs hurt or your throat aches, you think you'll never be glad again. With Jesus to help you, you can be happy. He loves and cares about you. He knows when you hurt and He feels bad. He loves you." She sang three more songs that told the story of Jesus and His love.

When Melody finished singing, it was so still in the room that a nurse poked her head in the door to see if all was well. Suddenly the children burst out clapping and wouldn't quit until Melody sang another song.

She beamed with pleasure. Her heart almost burst with joy. Happiness was singing to the children.

The boys and girls were reluctant to go back to their rooms until Miss Jenkins told them that Melody and Matt were coming back after supper.

"You did a beautiful job," praised Miss Jenkins as they walked to the elevator. Melody was on one side of her and Matt with the guitar, on the other side. "If I can manage it how would you like to return once a week? When General hears about you I know they'll be after you to sing for their children. Would you be interested?"

"I'll say," exclaimed Melody breathlessly. "How about it, Matt?"

"Maybe," he said gruffly. He wouldn't meet her eyes.

Melody answered Miss Jenkins' questions as they rode down the elevator. She glanced at Matt from time to time, wondering why he looked so angry. He'd done a beautiful job entertaining.

"Would it be all right to leave my guitar here?" asked Melody as they stopped at the front door.

"Of course. I'll put it in the nurses' lounge," said Miss Jenkins, taking the case from Matt. "I'll see you after a while." She hurried away down the hall, her shoes making a whisper on the polished floors.

Matt shoved open the large plate glass door and would have let it crash against Melody if she hadn't caught it in time.

She hurried after him as he strode to the car in the parking lot.

"What's the matter, Matt?" she asked when they reached the car.

"I'm going back to the ranch," he said gruffly. "You can find your own way home."

"Why?"

He turned on her angrily. "I'll take no part in that religious mumbo jumbo you crammed down their throats. They are stuck in that miserable hospital, yet you have the nerve to tell them they can be happy and trust Jesus to help them."

"Matt!" she exclaimed, grasping his arm and staring up at him. "I'm surprised at you. Jesus is the answer to everything. You should know that. You've heard it all your life."

"I've heard it, but you don't think I believed it, do you? Well, I sure don't. I've gotten along fine on my own. I'm not going to depend on that fairy tale stuff you tried to push off on the kids."

"You should be ashamed of yourself."

"I know. I should have told the kids you were lying. I almost did."

"It's a good thing you didn't, Matthew Chamberlain!" she said, shaking his arm. "Those kids need to know that Jesus loves them. They need to believe it."

Matt jerked himself free. "I'm leaving."

"You can't leave me stranded. It's twenty miles home and no way to get there. You can't leave me!"

"Can't I? I have the car keys." He jangled them under her nose.

She grabbed for them and missed. "You wouldn't be so mean."

"Wouldn't I? I'll see you at the ranch." He jumped in and started the motor with a roar.

"Matt! How will I get home?"

"Come now."

"I can't."

"Then walk."

Melody leaped out of the way as Matt backed the car out and drove off, squealing the tires.

With her hands on her hips she stared after him. Now what? How could he be so mean?

With a sigh she turned and walked toward the hospital door. At least her guitar was safe inside. She could do the evening performance alone. It wouldn't be as good without Matt but she'd do her best.

Matt! That mean, rotten guy!

6

Jealousy

AFTER A SUCCESSFUL evening performance Melody was dialing home from the pay phone in the hall when Matt sauntered toward her.

"I see you changed your mind," she said, hanging up with a bang. She stood with her hands on her hips, her eyes blazing.

"I didn't think I'd better go without Melody of love and brightness so I came back." He spoke lightly with a hesitant smile.

"Thanks," she said sarcastically, reaching for the guitar.

"I'll carry it."

"You're the very epitome of kindness."

They walked in angry silence to the car. Matt put the guitar in the backseat while Melody slid into the front, slamming the door.

"You don't like me very much, do you, Melody?" he asked as he slid under the steering wheel.

"Not much."

"What about this 'love your brother' bit?"

'In your case it's pretty hard."

Matt revved up the motor and roared out of the parking lot.

"Grow up, Matt," snapped Melody, grabbing the dash for support as they turned onto the highway.

"Shut up!"

"I can talk if I please. Does it upset poor itty bitty baby Matt when I tell him to grow up?"

Matt slammed on the brakes, spinning the car around. He pulled it back under control and stopped at the side of the road. "See you around, smarty." He opened the door to get out.

Melody grabbed his arm. "Don't, Matt! I'm sorry for being so rotten to you. I really am. Please, Matt." She sure hadn't acted like a Christian.

Matt sat rigid, staring straight ahead.

"I'm really sorry, Matt," she said softly.

He pulled the door shut and slumped against the steering wheel. "I know I'm no good."

She slid close to him and put her hand on his head. "You need Jesus, Matt."

He jerked up, glaring at her. "I don't!"

"I won't say any more right now, Matt," she said with a sigh. She slid back across the seat and leaned her head back, her eyes closed. "Let's go home."

"Anything for Melody of love," he said lightly as he drove back on the highway.

They rode in silence for about five minutes.

"Do you realize how much happiness we brought those kids today?" asked Melody, turning toward Matt.

"It wasn't bad, was it?" he asked with a grin. "For a while there I really thought I was somebody worthwhile. The way the kids looked at me and all. They really liked me. And all that applause."

"We're invited to sing once a week."

"Could you leave out the religious stuff?"

"No."

"I'll have no part of that."

"You can help me with the other part and I'll carry the gospel songs and the story alone. Does that suit you?"

"Maybe. I'll give it some thought." He passed a slow-moving tractor. "Did you notice that blond boy? His name is Joey. He told me he loved me. Doesn't that get you? He wanted to kiss me good-by but I told him we'd shake hands. Funny, isn't it? That little kid made me feel better than I've ever felt. He really did love me. I can't get over that."

Melody smiled but made no comment. She was afraid she'd offend him and upset his mood. She looked out the window at the hilly ranchland. Birds lit on fence posts and then up and away. Cattle dotted the grassy pasture. The sun was low in the sky. With daylight saving time it didn't get dark until after ten o'clock. She looked at her watch. She'd still have time to check her foal.

"Are you going to tell your folks about that dumb stunt I pulled?" asked Matt sharply.

"No. Should I?" she asked, looking at him and smiling.

"I don't want you to," he said stiffly.

"I won't."

"Thanks. You really are Melody of love, aren't you?"

"Guess so," she answered with a shrug. "Plus beau-

tiful, adorable, and a hard worker. And we can't forget the most terrific singer in the nation."

"No conceit at all."

"Just pure truth, boy. Just pure truth."

They were laughing as Matt drove under the arch-
way and around the circle drive. He parked in front of
the garage.

"I'm going to check Misty and my foal before I go
in," said Melody, opening the car door and getting out.
"Go tell Mom I'll be right in."

"OK. I'll give her the car keys. She doesn't make
me nervous like your dad does." Matt walked into the
house, banging the door.

Melody walked slowly toward the barn, enjoying the
smell of freshly cut hay. Touser whined, wagging his
tail vigorously.

Melody stepped into the barn, flipping the light on.
She walked to Misty's stall and looked in. "How's my
baby? Come here, Misty." She held her hand out and
Misty nuzzled it.

"I heard you drive in and come down here," said
Wade from behind her.

She spun around and hugged him eagerly. "Oh,
Wade, we sang for the children in the hospital. It was
so exciting and Matt did a beautiful job."

Wade jerked back. "Did he?" asked Wade coldly.

"We're going once a week. The children loved us."

"And you love Matt."

"Wade! How can you say that?" snapped Melody,
her hands on her hips. "I love you."

"It seems all your time is taken up with Matt," said

Wade through clenched teeth. "Can't you find time for me? We used to have lots of fun."

"This summer is different. You know that. All my beautiful plans were messed up. Can I help it if life isn't easy anymore? I didn't choose the summer to be like this, did I?" Tears filled her eyes and she turned away from Wade. She walked out of the barn. The outside yard light gave off enough light for her to see the path to the house.

"I'm sorry, Melody," said Wade, catching her arm. He turned her to him and held her close. "I know this has been a hard time for you. I should be more patient. I hate to admit it but I'm human too. I mean I really have been too human lately. I get so angry and impatient all the time. I can't believe myself."

Melody looked up at him, tears sparkling in her eyes. "I can't seem to control my emotions either. I get angry so easily and I used to never lose my temper. Almost never," she added with a grin. "Now, it's hard to think of myself as a good Christian."

"I know how you feel, Melody. I always thought I was a great Christian. Now, I find out when troubles come along I'm not all that great. I haven't been praying as much as usual or reading my Bible. When I start to pray I think about you and Matt together and I get so angry and jealous that I can't pray."

"I'm sorry, Wade," she said softly. "You have nothing to be jealous about."

"I believe it when you tell me, but as soon as monster Matt's around I forget."

"We're both having a rotten summer, aren't we?"

"Just different, Melody. If we could make the best of it, it wouldn't seem so bad. My dad always says to make the best of a bad situation because something good will come of it."

"What good have I done this summer?" asked Melody sadly.

"You're doing a lot. You do all your mother's work plus your own."

"Not willingly, Wade. I can't seem to help it."

Just then Matt stepped out of the shadows. "What's taking so long, Melody?"

"She's talking with me," said Wade, tightening his arms around her.

"Randy wants you," said Matt softly.

"I'll be right in," answered Melody with a sigh.

"I'm sure Betty can manage Randy a little longer," snapped Wade.

"He's crying," said Matt stiffly.

"Then you take care of him," growled Wade. "You're so good at it."

"It really gripes you that I'm better at some things, doesn't it, cowboy?"

"No more than it gripes you because I can do most things better, dude."

"Wade!" cried Melody, pulling free. "Matt! Stop fighting!"

"Keep out of this, Melody," snapped Wade, glaring at Matt. "He's been after a fight ever since he came. I'm ready if he is."

"Don't you dare fight or I'll never speak to you again, Wade Everett!"

"Are you afraid I'll hurt fancy pants?"

"Don't call me names," growled Matt, advancing with his fists doubled.

"This is too ridiculous!" said Melody impatiently. "Come on, Matt. Let's go in." She took his hand.

"Take the baby in so the big bully won't hurt him," said Wade.

"What baby?" hissed Matt, jerking his hand from Melody and pushing his face close to Wade's. "You're jealous. That's your problem."

"Me? Jealous of a fancy pants like you? I've nothing to be jealous of. Melody's not dumb enough to fall for you."

Melody clenched her fists, angry sparks shooting from her eyes. "I hate you both!"

Just then Betty dashed out of the house. "Come in, you guys. I fixed cake and ice cream for you."

"I don't want any," said Wade. He stepped close to Melody. "Come for a walk with me."

"Not tonight, Wade," she said stiffly.

"She's going to have a dish of ice cream with me," said Matt triumphantly.

"No I'm not! I'm going to my room and I don't want to hear anything out of anybody." Melody dashed into the house. What a way for a great day to end. Wouldn't things ever be the same again?

7

Letter from Mexico

THE HOT AUGUST SUN beat down on Melody as she
opened the mailbox and took out the mail. She shuffled
through it until she found her weekly letter from Aunt
Lucy. She stared sadly at the Mexican address. How
could she stand to read another glowing report from
the trio?

Slowly she walked along the circle drive toward
the house. It was hard to share the letters with her
family. They never seemed to notice what an effort it
was to keep the tears back. Wade noticed when he
wasn't angry with her.

She sighed as she reached up and picked an elm leaf
off a tree. It had been a week since she'd stormed into
the house, declaring that she hated both Wade and
Matt. During that week Wade had kept busy so that
he could avoid her. Matt had been his usual self, sometimes nice, sometimes rotten. He drove to town by
himself several times without any explanations.

It was a relief to get back in the air conditioned
house. Melody laid the mail on Mr. Robins' desk in the

study then went to the bathroom, washed her face with cold water, and hurried to her bedroom. She flopped on her stomach across her bed and tore open the letter from Aunt Lucy.

She asked about Randy and said how much she missed him. Melody skimmed over that part until she came to the section about the trio.

"Melody, you would be thrilled at the number of souls that have accepted Christ through the ministry of song and Ben's preaching. These people are hungry for God. The meeting places have been packed. People crowd on the outside and peek in the windows. In one small town we had some trouble with the Catholic priest. He forbade all his people to go to the church to hear the music. One very timid lady stopped us on the street the day we arrived and told us that they'd heard from the neighboring village that we were coming. And she said their Padre had refused to let them attend the gospel sing. Our hearts were broken for the poor souls. Think of their bondage! They were so hungry to hear the Gospel songs, so we had the most inspiring thought that I know came from God. We asked for permission from the town officials to hold the meeting in the small park. It was a shady, quiet place and perfect because we could set up our mikes, and with Bev on the guitar we could be heard beautifully. Needless to say, the priest paid us a visit. He was very angry. He told us that he didn't like what we were doing and he would do everything in his power to make us leave. Ben was as kind as he could be but he remained firm. Ben told him we'd come to sing and preach and that's just what we intended to do. To make a long story short, Melody, that priest listened to our songs and our sermons, and on the third night we were there he marched up in front of everyone and announced that he wanted to accept Jesus as his personal Saviour. Not a dry eye was present. He apologized publicly for disturbing us and for not allowing his people to attend. He begged us to stay another day so he could persuade his people to come listen and that they had his permission to accept this Christ as a personal Saviour. Of course we agreed. Souls are more important than a schedule. More people attended that night than in any other meeting. At least twenty-five accepted Christ that night. We were so happy it was hard to sing without bursting into tears. And best of all there is a gospel church in that village so the new Christians will be fed. In many of the places we had to leave knowing that the new believers might never again hear a gospel service. It really is heartbreaking.

"Bev was sick a few days but not enough to keep her from singing. So far none of the rest of us have been down. It is so hot here that we must follow the custom of a daily siesta. But of course we don't mind.

"We're bringing something back for you, Melody. I know it won't take the place of the trip but you'll know we've thought about you and remembered to pray for you. The Lord will bless you for helping your folks this summer and most important to me—taking care of my Randy."

Aunt Lucy went on to say more about the trip from village to village and then ended the letter.

Melody flung the letter across the room and buried her face in her pillow and cried until it was soggy. How unfair! She should have been on the trip playing her guitar and singing with the trio and watching souls being saved and blessed. Instead she had to stay home and work, work, work! Not only that. She and Wade were growing farther and farther apart. How could life be so terrible? What had she done to the Lord to be punished so? What was the valuable lesson she was supposed to learn?

Finally Melody pushed herself off the bed, wiped her tears away and blew her nose. The reflection in the mirror of the blonde girl made her cover her face and cry again.

"No more crying," she told herself sternly. "All it gets me is a headache." She wiped her tears and blew her nose. She looked at her watch. It was time to fix dinner.

She hurried to the bathroom and washed her face, brushed her hair, and tried to smile.

"What's for dinner?" asked Betty as Melody entered the kitchen.

"Who wants to know?" snapped Melody. Then she could've bitten off her tongue. Why couldn't she control herself?

"I want to know, smarty. What's the matter with you anyway? You look terrible."

"Thanks." Melody took the potatoes out of the bin. "Where's Randy? I thought it was your turn to watch him."

"Matt has him. He finished his work early, so he said he'd take Randy for a walk. For a rotten guy he can be pretty nice at times."

"He can, can't he? I'd like to see him be nice all the time."

"Then he wouldn't be Matt."

"He'd be a better Matt," said Melody, peeling the potatoes and cutting them into small pieces. She put them on to boil then took hamburger out of the refrigerator.

"Good. Hamburger patties," said Betty as she watched Melody mix the ingredients together. "I love 'em."

Melody forced herself to be friendly with Betty as she fixed dinner. While she was tossing the salad, Matt came in with Randy.

"Call me when dinner's ready," said Betty, dashing away.

"Randy's hungry," said Matt, lifting the baby into the highchair. "I'll feed him now and put him down for his nap."

"That's too good to be true," said Melody, clasping her hands against her chest. "I get so tired trying to keep dinner running smoothly, feeding Randy and myself. Thanks, Matt."

He tipped her chin up and smiled into her eyes. "Think nothing of it, Melody of love."

Melody couldn't help smiling. At that moment she really liked Matt. "You will go tomorrow to sing at the hospital, won't you, Matt?" she asked.

He turned away with a shrug.

"You're so wonderful with them, Matt. And think of Joey. He'll be looking for you."

"Wade won't like it."

"I'll take care of Wade."

"Wish I could," Matt said grimly as he washed Randy's hands and face. He fixed Randy's lunch while Melody opened the corn and put it on to cook.

"Open wide, Randy," said Matt, holding a spoon of macaroni and beef out to him.

"If you can get him to eat that you're really a genius," said Melody, standing beside Matt's chair.

"A genius is born," said Matt as Randy took the bite and wanted more.

"You're great with kids. You should plan your future around them. You could be a pediatrician or an entertainer or a teacher."

"It really worries you, doesn't it?"

"What?"

"My future." Matt gave Randy a bite of the dutch apple dessert.

"Yes, it does. You have a talent that shouldn't be wasted. You have so much to give if you could just forget about feeling sorry for yourself."

"Is that what I do?" asked Matt coldly.

"I didn't say it to hurt your feelings, Matt. I really want to help," said Melody, laying her hand on Matt's shoulder. "I want to see you turn your life over to the Lord and ask Him to lead you. Just think what you could do to help your parents on the mission field. You could be with them, working with them."

"Do you think they'd want me?" sneered Matt.

"Sure they would."

"Then why did they send me away in the first place?"

"So you could go to school, wasn't it?"

Matt snapped the tray off the highchair and picked up Randy. "Let's get you to bed." He walked out without another word to Melody.

She turned back to dinner with a shrug. She must have overstepped into his private feelings again.

As she set the table she tried to think of ways that she could help Matt. She knew he liked her better maybe than he should. Could she use his feelings for her to persuade him to do better?

"Guess who's coming to dinner?" asked Wade, poking his head in the kitchen.

"Wade!" she exclaimed with a smile.

"Your dad thought I needed some cheering up. Which I do because I'm a rotten rat that can't keep his big mouth shut." He walked over to Melody and put his hands on her shoulders and looked deep into her eyes. "Do you forgive me?"

"Sure," she said, putting her arms around his waist. "And I'm sorry for getting upset. You know I don't hate you, don't you?"

"I was hoping you didn't. It almost killed me to stay away from you. I guess your dad knew we'd had a fight. I'm glad he asked me for dinner."

"Me too. How would you like to go with me tomorrow to the hospital? You could watch my great performance for the kids."

"I'd like to go." He bent his head to kiss her but was interrupted by Matt.

"I'm going too. The three of us. That should be very interesting," he said with a cocky grin.

"The more the merrier," said Wade cheerfully.

Melody was relieved that Wade was being friendly to Matt. If he would try to help Matt, maybe between them they could teach him to trust the Lord.

"I didn't mean to interrupt a kiss," said Matt. "We can't have Melody of love going kissless."

Before they knew what he intended Matt tipped Melody's face up and touched his lips to hers. She jumped back in surprise.

"Hey!" growled Wade, spinning Matt around. "That's my girl."

"Don't hit him," shrieked Melody, grabbing Wade's arm.

"She loves me," said Matt, leering at Wade.

"I just don't want blood all over the kitchen," said Melody, using all her strength to hang on to Wade's arm.

"We'll settle this another time," snapped Wade.

"Any time," said Matt, leaning against the counter.

Melody looked in exasperation from one to the other. "Sit down," she said in a tired voice. "Dad's coming now. It's time to eat."

8

Joey

IT WAS RAINING as they drove to the hospital. The gloom inside the car was heavier than the gloom outside.

Wade was driving, Melody sat in the middle and Matt next to her. Melody tried to sit as close to Wade as possible so he wouldn't think that she was overly friendly with Matt. Matt! What a dumb thing to do. Kiss her! And right in front of Wade. Of course that's the reason he did it. He wanted to antagonize Wade. She glanced up at him but he was keeping his attention on the road. She glanced at Matt. He winked at her, and she jerked her eyes back and stared straight ahead.

How could they help the children when the strain between them was so apparent? It would never do.

Melody took a deep breath, looking from one to the other. "OK, boys! Listen to me. We are going to the hospital to do good. How can we if you two are quarreling? Be friends, will you? Wade? Matt? For the kids?"

"You're right of course," agreed Wade, driving into the parking lot. "I won't cause any trouble."

"I won't either," said Matt, winking at Melody.

Melody frowned at him then glanced quickly at Wade to see if he'd caught the wink. He hadn't.

"I'll pull up by the door to let you out so you won't get wet," said Wade, stopping outside the entrance.

"I'll take the guitar," said Matt, jumping out and reaching for the guitar.

Melody slid across the seat and dashed to the door that Matt was holding open.

"I like that red dress," said Matt as they waited inside for Wade. "You look pretty in red."

"Why, thank you, Matt!" she said in surprise.

"What's the matter? Didn't you think I noticed what you look like?"

"Of course not."

"I always notice how pretty you are."

"Here comes Wade. Don't say anything to upset him." Melody waited by the door with a big smile for Wade. His red hair was wet from the rain. He was tall and slender with wide shoulders and narrow hips. Melody liked his dark brown pants and gold shirt.

"It's wet out there," said Wade, smiling.

"You don't say," said Matt dryly.

"Let's find Miss Jenkins and get going," said Melody, trying to ward off any unpleasantries. "There she is now." Melody indicated the gray-haired nurse standing by the elevators.

She turned and smiled as Melody, Wade, and Matt walked up.

"The children are waiting in eager anticipation,"

said Miss Jenkins. The elevator opened and they all stepped in. Matt held the guitar upright so it wouldn't bump anyone. Wade held Melody's hand.

"Miss Jenkins, this is Wade Everett. He's going to tell the children a story," said Melody.

"They'll love that," answered Miss Jenkins. She smiled at them. "It makes me feel so good to see that there are young people interested in doing good. You are three wonderful people to take out time to do this for the children."

"We love doing it," said Melody, her blue eyes shining with excitement.

"I know you do," said Miss Jenkins. "I can tell by just looking at you."

The elevator door opened and they stepped out and walked to the waiting children.

The children clapped so loud when they stepped into the room that Melody thought her heart would burst with happiness.

Matt took out the guitar and without any introduction he and Melody sang "Froggy Went A Courtin'." After that they sang "Old MacDonald Had a Farm." The children joined in boisterously.

Melody put her whole self into each song. When it was time to introduce Wade, she was bubbling with enthusiasm.

"Children, this redheaded guy came today to tell you a story that you'll never forget. He's been patiently waiting to talk while Matt and I sang, so we won't keep him waiting any longer." Melody held out her hand to Wade and he stepped up beside her, bow-ing to the children and smiling. "Children, Wade Everett."

The children clapped then sat quietly.

Wade told them about Jesus being their friend. He told them the story of the Good Shepherd, using pictures.

Melody looked from one sick child to the next. They were completely engrossed in the story.

To Melody's surprise Matt hadn't left when she'd started what he called the religious junk. He was sitting between two little girls, holding their hands. The biggest surprise was that he was listening to Wade's story too.

Melody breathed a prayer for Matt. He needed the Lord. She wanted to put her arms around him and tell him to put aside his bitterness and accept the love that Christ had for him.

After Wade prayed, Melody sang "Happiness Is the Lord." The children clapped and clapped, wanting more but it was time for them to go back to their own rooms.

Miss Jenkins walked down the corridor with Melody, Wade, and Matt. "You are coming back this evening, aren't you?" she asked as they stopped near the elevator.

"Oh, yes," breathed Melody.

"It was terrific," said Wade. "No wonder Melody is excited. I'd like to be included even if I don't take part."

"The children need to hear about God," said Miss Jenkins.

Matt snorted but didn't say anything.

Melody frowned at him as Miss Jenkins told them the good they were doing.

"Where's Joey?" asked Matt suddenly. "I didn't see him with the others."

"Poor Joey Ferguson," said Miss Jenkins sadly. "He was too ill to join the others. He wanted to so badly. I'm afraid he won't ever be able to. He's getting worse each day."

"You mean he's going to die?" asked Matt sharply.

"Yes."

"Why wasn't I told he was that sick?"

"I thought you knew. You spent so much time with him."

Melody looked at Matt in surprise. So that's where he'd gone.

"You can't help him at all?" asked Matt, gripping the guitar case so tightly that his knuckles were white.

"Nothing can be done."

Just then a distraught woman rushed down the corridor to them. "Matt! Matt! Joey's asking for you," she said, wringing her hands.

"Is he worse?" he asked huskily.

She clutched his arm and looked imploringly into his face. "Please hurry to see my Joey. He's been asking for you. He wants you!"

"What—what can I do?" asked Matt in a choked voice.

"He wants you!" exclaimed the woman, tugging at Matt's arm.

"Go with her," said Miss Jenkins. "Just being with Joey will help him."

"Melody?" asked Matt, begging her to help him.

"Mrs. Ferguson, may I come too?" asked Melody quietly.

"Of course. Both of you come see my Joey," cried Mrs. Ferguson.

"I'll meet you in the car," said Wade, picking up the guitar that Matt had plopped down.

"I'll take that and we can sing to him," said Melody, taking the guitar. She looked up at Wade and mouthed the words, "Pray for us."

Wade promised he would as he stepped into the elevator with Miss Jenkins.

Mrs. Ferguson led Melody and Matt to Joey's room. "You go in. I'll stay out here a while." She ran her hand through her disheveled hair.

"We'll help him," said Melody softly.

"Please do!"

"Just how can we?" growled Matt close to her ear as they walked through the door into Joey's room.

"Matt!" cried Joey, lifting his head off the pillow. "You came! I wanted you to come."

"Hi ya, buddy," greeted Matt, taking the small hand. "What's this? You didn't come to hear us sing."

"I couldn't, Matt. Can you sing for me anyway?"

"Of course we can," said Melody, handing the guitar to Matt. "What do you want to hear?"

"I don't care," said Joey, leaning against his pillow, looking at Matt with eyes full of love.

"How about 'The Bear Went Over the Mountain'? You like that, don't you?" Matt started the song before Joey could answer. He went from that to "Knick

Knack Paddy Whack" and onto other songs that made Joey laugh in delight.

"Can you sing 'Happiness and the Lord'?" asked Joey when Matt stopped for breath.

"You must mean 'Happiness Is the Lord,'" said Melody as Matt sent her a silent plea for help.

"Melody will sing it for you," said Matt, handing her the guitar. "I'm tired."

"I like to hear about Jesus," said Joey.

Melody sang the song then two others that she thought Joey would enjoy.

"It's time we left so you can rest, Joey," said Matt, tousling Joey's hair.

"Don't go!" wailed Joey, catching Matt's hand.

"But you're tired."

"I don't want you to leave. I'm scared!"

"Scared of what?" asked Melody.

Joey kept his eyes glued to Matt's face. "I'm going to die."

"What?" asked Matt in alarm.

"I am. I'm not supposed to know but I heard one of the nurses say so when she thought I was asleep. I don't want to die!" His voice rose until Melody became alarmed.

"Don't, Joey," said Matt, cradling the little boy in his arms. "Hush now. Hush. You'll be OK."

"But—but I won't. I'm going to—to—to die."

"Hush, Joey," said Matt with his face buried in Joey's blond hair. The two blonds blended, making it impossible to distinguish one from the other.

"I'm—I'm so—so scared, Matt."

"You don't have to be afraid," said Melody softly as

she walked around to the other side of the bed and took one of Joey's small hands. "Listen to me, Joey."

Matt pulled away from Joey. He dabbed his eyes and rubbed his hand across his nose. "Listen to her, Joey. She can help you. I can't." With that Matt turned and rushed from the room.

"Joey, I know about Someone who is your very best Friend. If I told you that when you die you can live with Him, would you be scared then?"

"I—I guess not," said Joey, turning his eyes from the closed door to Melody.

"Joey, do you know who Jesus is?"

"Sure I do." Joey smiled weakly. "He came down from heaven to be born at Christmas. And He's got something to do with Easter, too."

"Yes, He does. That was when He died on the cross so He could take away all the sin that keeps us away from God. Now anyone who believes in Jesus can become a child of God, and heaven will be his real home with Jesus forever."

Joey frowned. "Sin means bad things, doesn't it? I've done bad things, even here in the hospital. Can Jesus take away all my bad sins too? I'd like to belong to God and live with Him in heaven." Joey's eyes looked eagerly into Melody's. "Heaven is a beautiful place, isn't it?"

"Yes, it is, because God lives there and nothing bad is there—no sickness or pain or crying," Melody assured him.

"Are—are you sure it'll be like that?"

"The Bible tells us that it will be. The Bible is God's Word and it doesn't tell lies. Heaven is the home where Jesus is. He really will be glad to see you, Joey."

"But how do I know that Jesus is my Friend and that He will let me live in heaven?" asked Joey, big tears in his eyes.

"Jesus is your very best Friend and loves you very much. He has promised that, if you believe in Him, He will take you to heaven to live with Him. Jesus always keeps His promises."

"I do believe in Jesus and I really want to live in heaven. How can I tell Him?"

"We'll talk to Jesus right now. Praying is talking with Jesus." Melody bowed her head beside Joey's and she prayed for Joey to trust Jesus and to be ready to live in heaven with Him. When she finished praying she looked into Joey's eyes. "Do you want to talk to your Friend right now, Joey?"

Joey bowed his head and closed his eyes tight. "Jesus, I am glad you are my best Friend. Thank you for making a place in heaven for me. Help me not to be afraid to go live with You. Take care of Mom and Dad while I'm with You." He opened his eyes and smiled. "Thank you, Melody. I love you almost as much as I love Matt."

"I love you too, Joey." She kissed him on the cheek. "I'll see you later."

"Tell Matt not to be mad at me."

"He's not mad, Joey. He left because he didn't want you to see how he felt. He hasn't learned that Jesus is his best Friend. You pray for him, Joey. OK?"

"I will. Bye, Melody."

"Bye, Joey." She closed the door behind her then leaned against it as she wiped the tears from her eyes.

9

Shadow of Death

WADE WAS STANDING by the entrance door when Melody came down. He saw her get off the elevator and hurried to her.

"It's raining too hard out. Let's eat in the coffee shop," he said, searching her face.

"OK," mumbled Melody, interlocking her fingers with Wade's and leaning her head against his arm. "Oh, Wade. He's going to die! He's so young."

"Joey?"

"Yes. But I did help him. I told him about Jesus." She looked up into Wade's concerned face. "Now, who will help me? And Joey's parents? And even poor Matt. He's so torn up about it."

"Let's go sit down," said Wade, leading her to a secluded spot in the lounge. They sat on a bright orange sofa. "I'll see if I can help Joey's parents. They need the Lord to help them, especially right now."

"Where's Matt?" asked Melody, looking around with a frown.

"I don't know. He didn't come this way or I would've stopped him at the door."

"Joey begged him to help him but Matt couldn't, so he ran out. He needs the Lord, Wade. That's why I've been helping him this summer. He has a special feeling for me and I think he listens to me."

"A special feeling of love," growled Wade.

Melody put her free hand against Wade's cheek. "It's not love the way you mean it, Wade. We're friends. He doesn't love me anymore than I love him. I love you, Wade."

"Do you, Melody?" he asked, his eyes begging her to tell the truth.

"Yes."

"You don't just feel sorry for me because we're friends from kid days?"

"No. I love you for you right now."

"I've been such an idiot, Melody. Forgive me." Wade leaned back, Melody's hand in his. "You'd think since I'm going to be a minister I'd know how to handle my feelings. But, wow! I found out just how human I am."

"Don't apologize, Wade. I understand."

"I really thought since God has a special purpose for me that I was above jealousy and all that. But, you know, Melody, I'm not. Only with God's help can I overcome." He pushed his fingers through his hair. "Forgive me, Melody."

"Oh, Wade," she whispered, a lump in her throat and tears stinging her eyes. "No wonder God can use you. You know how to surrender to Him."

"So, this is where you two disappeared to," growled Matt. "You're so wrapped up with yourselves that you can't remember there's a little boy dying upstairs."

Melody jumped up, holding her hand out to Matt. "Sit down, Matt." Her heart went out to him. How he was suffering! "I prayed with Joey. He feels ready to live with Jesus."

"How does that help?" asked Matt angrily.

"Sit down, Matt," said Wade firmly. "You're upset. If you don't quiet down, you'll get kicked out of here."

Matt plopped into a chair opposite the sofa where Melody and Wade sat. A tall, broad-leafed plant hid Matt from the others in the room. Matt covered his face with his hands and slouched forward in the chair.

"Dying is part of life," said Melody. "It's hard on us but we must accept it, Matt."

He groaned louder.

Melody looked imploringly at Wade.

"Do you want—us to—to pray for you?" asked Wade.

"Pray!" exclaimed Matt, leaping to his feet and glaring at them. "I don't want you or anyone to pray for me!" He stood with his feet apart, his fists clenched. "Can't you leave me alone?"

"Oh, Matt," said Melody, jumping up and putting her arm around him. "Matt, we only want to help you." He was such a little boy at times.

He jerked away from her. "Nobody can help me."

Just then Miss Jenkins came hurrying across the room to them. "Matt! Thank goodness I found you. I was on my way to the coffee shop in hopes you'd be there."

"What's wrong?" asked Melody in alarm.

"It's Joey Ferguson again. He's much worse. He keeps asking for Matt. His parents are with him, but he insists on seeing you. Please come." Miss Jenkins gripped her hands together in front of her and begged Matt with her whole being.

"No. I can't," gasped Matt in agony. "I can't go watch him die."

"Think of someone besides yourself for a change," said Wade sharply. "That little boy needs you, Matt. Think of him."

"I'll go with you, Matt," said Melody, taking his hand.

"And I'll go talk to the parents. They need help now too." Wade walked with Miss Jenkins toward the elevator.

Melody tugged gently on Matt's hand. "Let's go help Joey."

"I can't," groaned Matt, pushing his fingers through his blond hair.

"Yes, you can!" said Melody.

"I can't talk to him about Jesus or heaven."

"Just be there. I'll talk if he needs me to."

They hurried to the waiting elevator and stepped in. No one spoke as it ascended.

Mr. and Mrs. Ferguson were standing beside Joey's bed when they entered his room.

"Matt!" exclaimed Joey in a frail voice. "You came."

"Joey, buddy. How's it going?" asked Matt, sitting on a chair close to the bed and taking Joey's frail hand.

"We'll see you later, Joey," said Mr. Ferguson, leading his wife from the room.

Wade joined them and asked if he could talk to them a while. The door closed behind them, leaving Melody, Matt, and Joey in the room.

"Hey, Joey, I know a funny story," said Matt as cheerfully as he could. "Want to hear it?"

"Not now, Matt," said Joey in a weak voice. "Tell me about living with Jesus in heaven. Tell me how it will be, so I won't be afraid."

"A big boy like you shouldn't be afraid of anything," said Matt, ruffling Joey's hair.

Melody turned toward the window and looked out. Tears blinded her eyes so she couldn't see. How could she think missing a trip to Mexico was the worst thing that could happen to anybody? Right now she was facing real sorrow.

"Aren't you afraid of anything?" asked Joey.

"Of course not," bragged Matt.

"Not anything at all?"

"Maybe. I guess if a tiger leaped out of the closet over there and growled at me, I'd be afraid."

"Oh, Matt," said Joey, chuckling weakly. "There's no tiger in the hospital. Not lions or bears or anything."

"I know that."

"I guess there aren't even mice in here."

"Now, that's a good thing because I think Melody's afraid of mice."

Melody turned from the window with a smile. "Oh, no, I'm not afraid of mice. I'm lots bigger than a mouse."

"I'll say," said Matt, looking her up and down and making Joey laugh.

"Matt, now will you tell me about heaven?" asked Joey, clinging more tightly to Matt's hand.

"I—I can't, Joey. I can't!"

"Please, Matt. Please!"

"Aw, Joey!"

"Matt!" Joey clung with both hands to Matt.

"I'll tell you," said Melody, putting her hand over Joey's and Matt's. "Listen to this, Joey. Jesus loves you in a way that no one ever loved you before. He is waiting in heaven to put His arms around you and hold you and tell you He loves you. He'll give you a wonderful welcome, Joey."

"Is that right, Matt?" asked Joey.

"Yes," said Matt in a strangled voice.

"You don't sound like you believe it, Matt," whispered Joey, fear showing in his eyes. "Help me not to be scared. I want to be brave but I can't!"

"Joey! Joey!" whispered Matt in anguish, leaning his head on Joey's hand.

Joey put his arms around Matt's head, hugging him the best he could in his weakened condition.

Melody felt the tears sting her eyelids. A large lump lodged in her throat.

Just then the door opened and a nurse told them they would have to leave.

"Shake hands with me, Matt," said Joey.

"How about a kiss instead?" Matt cradled Joey in his arms and kissed him on each cheek. Joey kissed him.

"See you later, Matt," he said.

"See you later, Joey," said Matt.

"How about a kiss for me?" asked Melody, bending over Joey and kissing him.

"See you, Melody," Joey said with a smile.

Matt stumbled from the room. He stopped outside the door, leaning against the wall, tears streaming unheeded down his cheeks.

Melody stood beside him, not knowing if she should say something or if she should stay quiet.

"I couldn't help him at all," groaned Matt. "I couldn't say one thing to him to help him." He pulled out his hanky and blew his nose and wiped his face. "Joey's going to die! Why couldn't I say something, anything to make him happy?"

Melody took his hand, and they walked slowly down the corridor. "It's almost time for the program. We must put on a happy face for the kids."

"Do you think I can sing now? How can I pretend that all is well when just down the hall a little boy is dying? I won't do it, Melody." He jerked his hand away and raced to the elevator.

When the elevator stopped, Wade got off and Matt got on. Wade stared after him then spotted Melody and hurried to her side.

"What's wrong?" he asked, jerking his thumb toward the elevator.

"He feels bad about Joey. I—I do too."

Wade put his arm around her and led her to a bench in the corridor. They sat down. "I led Joey's parents to the Lord. They were both brought up in Christian homes but had never made a personal commitment to the Lord."

"Oh, Wade!" she said, looking at him with shining eyes. "I'm so glad!"

"You know something, Melody. Maybe you missed the trip to Mexico just so that the Ferguson family

could find Christ. If you hadn't been around to entertain the kids, we wouldn't have known about Joey. If
we wouldn't have known about Joey, we'd have never
met his parents."

"You could be right, Wade." She took a deep
breath. "I'd better wash my face and get ready for the
evening performance." She looked at her watch. "It's
time."

"Is Matt coming back?"

"No. We'll carry on ourselves."

Wade rubbed the back of her hand with his finger-
tip. "You mean you'll have to carry on. I'll tell a story
but I sure can't sing."

She squeezed his hand then stood up. "I'd better
hurry."

"I'll get your guitar and meet you outside the sunroom door."

"Thanks, Wade." Melody hurried down the corridor
thinking with part of her mind about the songs she
would sing and wondering about Matt with the other
part.

A few minutes later she joined Wade by the sunroom door. Miss Jenkins rushed up to them.

"The children are waiting," she said breathlessly.

"We're ready," said Melody, smiling until she felt
the smile reach her eyes.

The program went smoothly but the kids asked about
Matt and said they really missed him.

Melody's throat was dry by the time she finished the
last song and said the last good-by. She and Wade
left the room first and the children's applause followed
them down the corridor to the elevator.

"You look tired," said Wade as they rode down the elevator.

"I am," she said, leaning against the handrail.

"You did a great job."

"So did you. They loved that story."

The elevator stopped, the doors opened and they stepped out.

"I wonder if it's still raining," said Wade as they reached the outside door. He looked out. "Sure is."

"I hope Matt's in the car," said Melody.

"Do you want to wait here and let me drive up for you?"

"No. I won't melt." She followed Wade out. They ran hand in hand to the car across the parking lot.

Wade opened the door and shoved the guitar in the backseat. Matt was sitting slumped forward. He lifted his head and looked at them. His eyes were red-rimmed, his face sorrowful.

Melody was just ready to get in when she heard someone shout her name. She turned and watched Miss Jenkins dash across the parking lot, a bubble umbrella over her head.

"I thought you would want to know about Joey Ferguson," she said when she reached the car.

Matt leaned his head out. "What about Joey?"

"He died about two minutes ago."

"Oh, no!" moaned Matt, sinking back against the seat.

"His parents are taking it better than I thought they would. They said they knew he was in good hands now. I'd like to see others take death that way. It's good if they believe in heaven after death. It's not so frightening."

"Thanks for telling us," said Melody. Tears blended with the rain and ran down her face.

"See you next week," said Miss Jenkins.

Melody slid into the car seat and sat as close to Wade as she could. It helped to touch him.

Wade put his arm around her. "I'm glad we helped them."

"Helped!" gasped Matt. "What kind of help did we give? None!"

10

Telephone Call to Peru

MELODY LEANED against the rail fence, looking over it at the horses in the corral. Misty and her foal, Rina and her filly were romping around.

"Where's Randy?" asked Betty, joining her sister.

"Taking a nap finally. It gave me time to come look at them." Melody pointed to the horses.

"Don't they look cute in their halters? I love to stand here and watch them play."

"Me too." She sighed. "I haven't had as much time to be around my foal as I'd like. And there's been no time to ride. I miss that so much."

"Melody?"

"Yes?"

"What's up with monster Matt? He's been so quiet and different these past two days." Betty leaned against the fence, looking at Melody with a frown.

"Joey's death hit him pretty hard. He really loved that kid."

"Melody, have you noticed how different things were this summer?"

"I'll say." She pushed her hair back from her hot face.

"Our family once was a happy family. Now, we aren't always."

"It's been my fault mostly," admitted Melody. "I was so upset about not going to Mexico that I really acted rotten. I think I learned my lesson."

"What?"

"To be a sweet Christian no matter what." She turned around and hooked her elbows over the top rail and propped one foot on the bottom rail. "A person can't take being a Christian for granted. You have to work at it by constant living for Jesus, reading the Bible, and praying."

"You're beginning to sound like Wade," said Betty, chuckling.

Melody laughed with her. "I guess I am."

A sudden wind sent a dust devil swirling across the corral.

"Oh, oh. Here comes monster Matt. I'll be shoving off." Betty dashed away toward the cook shack.

"I thought you were going with Dad and Dave out on the range," said Melody as Matt stopped beside her.

"I didn't feel good," he said sullenly. He leaned against the fence, his chin against his hands.

"Do you have the flu?" asked Melody in concern.

"No." He turned to her with a haggard face. "I dreamed about Joey again last night. I dreamed he was crying because I couldn't help him. He screamed and screamed that he was afraid to die and that I

should tell him about heaven. I can't sleep anymore
without having terrible nightmares."

"Oh, Matt. You poor thing," said Melody, reaching
out to him.

He grabbed her hand and held it against his heart.
"Help me, Melody. You're the only person that can.
No one else really cares about me."

"Matt, what can I do?"

"Stand by me. Help me."

"You must help yourself, Matt. I can't do anything
for you." She rested her free hand on his shoulder.
"Matt, you need Jesus."

He dropped her hand and jumped back. "No!"

"He's the answer."

"Shut up! Do you hear me, Melody? Shut up!"

"Everybody in the county can hear you at that rate,"
she said. She walked away from him toward the house.

"Don't go," he said, catching her arm. "I'm sorry,
Melody. Honest. I won't yell again." He held her
hand as they walked around the house to the back
yard. They sat together on the big wooden swing
under the rose trellis.

"Aren't the flowers beautiful?" asked Melody, break-
ing off a yellow rose and smelling it. She held it out to
Matt.

He took it and stuck it in his hair. "How's that?"

She shrugged. "I've seen better."

"You have? I thought I couldn't be beat." He pulled
the flower out and tucked it in her hair. "Very pretty."

The swing moved back and forth in a gentle rhythm.
A meadow lark perched on a nearby post and sang.

"Summer's almost gone," said Matt, sighing loudly. "I may never see you again, Melody."

"You know where I live."

"I don't think your family would agree to another visit from monster Matt."

"I'm sorry about that nickname."

"I deserve it."

"You're right," she said with a wicked grin. "All those terrible things you did."

"I'm sorry, Melody. I wish the summer could start again so I could be different."

Melody looked off across the rolling pasture, her heart aching for him. Why couldn't he see that he couldn't change himself? Didn't he know that God working from the inside was the only one who could change him? She wanted to tell him so badly, but she knew he wouldn't listen. She squeezed his hand tight, closed her eyes and prayed from deep within that God would touch his heart and help him understand.

"What's the matter, Melody?" asked Matt softly.

"Nothing," she whispered as a tear slipped down her tanned cheek.

"You're crying!"

"I'm OK."

"What is it, Melody?" he asked gently. "What's wrong with Melody of love?"

She opened her eyes and looked deep into his. "I can't stand to see you bitter against God. I want you to love Him. I want you to find peace and happiness." Silently she prayed for guidance. For once he sat quietly and didn't interrupt her. "I've learned to love you, Matt. You're like family to me. I could cry when I see how sad you always are."

Matt pulled his hand free and wiped across his eyes. "Nobody really cares about me," he said in a strangled voice.

"I do. But, Matt, more important, God does. Romans 5:8 says, 'But God showed His *great* love for us by sending Christ to die for us while we were still sinners.' Think of it, Matt! God loves you that much!" Please, Lord, she prayed urgently, touch his heart. She told him of mankind's sin, of his sin, and how God had through love sent Jesus to die for everyone's sin so that all might live.

Matt brushed his hand down his pant leg then sat with his hand on his knee.

Because he still didn't object, Melody continued earnestly. "Ephesians 2:8 and 9 says, 'because of His kindness you have been saved through trusting Christ. And even trusting is not of yourselves; it too is a gift from God. Salvation is not a reward for the good we have done, so none of us can take credit for it.'" Melody clasped her hands tightly, tears sparkling in her eyes. Matt was really listening! Please, Lord, please! "Listen, Matt, to verse ten. 'It is God Himself who has made us what we are and given us new lives from Christ Jesus; and long ages ago He planned that we should spend these lives in helping others.' Can't you see, Matt? Your parents didn't desert you. They had to spend their lives in helping others. God wants your life so you can use it for Him."

"Melody. Matt. Am I interrupting?" asked Wade,

walking around the rose trellis and standing beside the swing.

Melody's heart dropped. What poor timing on Wade's part. Now maybe she'd completely lost Matt's attention.

"I thought you were out in the hot hay field," said Matt sharply.

"I was but I had to come up for a rake tine and I thought this would be a good time to find you, Matt."

"To work?" asked Matt bitterly.

"No. To apologize." He sank down on the grass near the swing, looking earnestly at Matt.

Melody smiled, her heart light.

"Why should you apologize to me?" asked Matt suspiciously.

"Because I've acted wrong." He shifted his weight, crossed his arms over his knees and continued. "I'm a Christian, Matt, and I should know better. I'm sorry for being mean and hateful. Can you forgive me?"

Melody thought she would burst with pride. She knew how much it took for Wade to apologize.

Matt shook his head in bewilderment. "You neither one can be for real. I'm the one that's been rotten."

"In Romans chapter three the Scriptures say that no one is good, that all have done wrong, but God has shown us a way to stop being guilty," said Wade earnestly. "If we put our trust in Jesus Christ and ask Him to take our sins upon Himself He will do just that."

Melody felt Matt stiffen, but still he remained quiet. She caught Wade's eye and smiled.

"Romans 10:9 and 10 say, 'For if you tell others with your own mouth that Jesus Christ is your Lord, and believe in your own heart that God has raised Him from the dead, you will be saved. For it is by believing in his heart that a man becomes right with God; and with his mouth he tells others of his faith, confirming his salvation.'" Wade took a deep breath, leaning toward Matt. "God wants to take away all your heartache and bitterness and replace it with love."

"God loves you, Matt," said Melody softly.

"No! He doesn't! How can He?" Matt covered his face with his hands.

"Matt, you've probably heard John 3:16 all your life but I'll quote it again," said Melody. "For God loved the world so much that He gave His only Son so that anyone who believes in Him shall not perish but have eternal life." She told Matt how much God loved him to make the way of salvation for him.

They talked to Matt, quoting Scriptures until Melody's mouth felt dry. She could feel the strong presence of God with them.

Finally they sat quietly, the buzz of a bumble bee the only sound.

"It all makes sense," said Matt slowly. "It's as if I have a new brain telling me the meanings of the Scriptures. It's amazing. I've heard the plan of salvation all my life and I never grasped it."

"Do you want us to pray with you?" asked Melody softly, her heart racing, her eyes filling with tears.

"Yes. Yes, I do," said Matt.

Melody felt as if she would burst with joy as they

prayed. Wade prayed, then Melody, and then Matt. His words stumbled out but were straight from his heart.

Tears flowed unchecked down Melody's tanned cheeks. It felt so good to lead someone to Christ. She started singing "Thank You, Lord, for Saving My Soul," and Matt joined in, their voices blending beautifully.

Tears slid down Matt's cheeks. He pulled out his hanky and wiped them off then blew his nose. "Why couldn't I have accepted Christ in time to help Joey?"

"There are a lot of Joeys in the world," said Wade. "You can do something special for all of them."

"Tomorrow's Joey's funeral," said Melody. "Mrs. Ferguson wants us to sing."

"It—it will be hard," said Matt, clearing his throat.

"Will you sing with me?" asked Melody, touching his hand.

He took a deep breath and slowly let it out. "Yes. Yes, we'll sing a song that will tell others of God's great love."

"Good for you," said Wade, jumping up. He grasped Matt's hand in a firm handshake. "I'm glad you accepted the Lord as your personal Saviour."

"Thanks for your help," said Matt, grinning.

"Hey, I've got to get that fork tine back to the hay-field. See you all later."

Melody watched him run around the house, his red hair bright in the sunlight.

They walked side by side around to the kitchen door.

"Forgive me for being so rotten this summer," said Matt as they stepped into the house.

"Were you rotten? I can't remember at all." She wrinkled her nose then smiled.

"Randy wants you, Melody," said Betty, hurrying in with Randy on her hip.

Randy squealed with delight when he saw Matt. He held his arms out to him and Matt with a happy smile took him from Betty.

"Amazing," said Betty, shaking her head. "I still can't get over that."

"Matt has just accepted Jesus as his Saviour," said Melody.

"You have, Matt? That's great! Really super!"

"We're going to tell Mom now," said Melody, leading the way. Betty joined the parade.

"Tell her, Matt," said Betty excitedly as they crowded into the bedroom.

Matt did. Mrs. Robins held her arms out to him, kissing him soundly. "That's the best news I've heard in a long time," she said, dabbing at the tears in her eyes. "Why don't you call your parents and tell them?"

"Should I? I mean, could I?" asked Matt, plopping Randy into Melody's arms.

"Can I listen in?" asked Betty. "I've always wanted to make a long, long, long distance phone call."

"Matt wants to talk in private," said Mrs. Robins, taking Betty's hand. "Don't bother him now."

"Do you think they'll want to hear from me?" asked Matt apprehensively.

"Call them, Matt," said Mrs. Robins, smiling lovingly. "They'll want to hear."

Matt bent and kissed her cheek then rushed out of the room.

"Monster Matt is gone for good I hope," said Betty. "You know, if I was old enough I just might fall for him."

"Fiddlesticks," said Mrs. Robins, causing Melody to laugh hard. "You are my baby and you are not going to date until you're at least thirty-five years old."

"Oh, Mom! I'm going to be a teenager in just ten days."

"But that doesn't mean you can date, young lady."

"I can dream."

"Dream but not date. Understand, Betty?"

Betty shrugged. "Sure, Mom."

Melody laughed again. "Mom, I think our Betty is growing up."

"It looks like Randy's the only baby in this house," said Mrs. Robins, smiling at her girls.

"It looks like it," said Melody, knowing that her mother meant that she was growing up too.

11

Melody of Love

MELODY AUTOMATICALLY dusted the piano. Her stomach cramped and tears stung her eyelids. Aunt Lucy and the trio were coming. How could she listen to their exciting stories and watch the slides without falling apart? Please help me, Lord. Give me a right attitude and a loving heart. Take away the bitterness.

She dusted the end tables. She couldn't excuse herself and go to her room because they were coming especially to show her the things they'd bought and the slides they'd taken. Sunday night they'd show and tell the church people.

She moved to the coffee table, wiping its smooth surface. She'd have to play it cool, that's all. She'd pretend to enjoy all the exciting news and shut her eyes to the slides. She couldn't break down in front of them. The tears that were trying to push themselves out would have to wait until she got to her room by herself. Oh, Lord, I need Your help desperately. She opened her eyes wide and swallowed hard.

"I'm finished in the kitchen," said Betty, rushing into the living room. "What next, Melody?"

"I don't know," snapped Melody. "Oh, Betty! I'm sorry. I'm just nervous."

"Do you think Aunt Lucy will bring me something too? Maybe a serape or a handmade straw bag. I can't wait until she comes. Won't she be surprised to see Randy walking? You didn't tell her when you wrote, did you? You promised you wouldn't."

Melody only half listened to Betty. She was trying to think out her grand performance for the evening. She would be cool and friendly and not show that she was upset about missing the heavenly trip. She'd even be nice to Bev, the girl who took her place.

"Is everything done, Melody?" asked Mrs. Robins, walking into the living room with the help of a cane.

"Mom! You're walking!" exclaimed Melody, dashing to her side.

"Mom!" shrieked Betty, dashing to the other side.

"I've been practicing," said Mrs. Robins, sinking down into a large green chair. "The doctor said I could but not to overdo it."

"I'm so glad to see you up," said Melody, sitting on the arm of the chair. "I think I'm going to cry."

"I know what you mean," said Mrs. Robins, smiling. "I was beginning to think I'd never walk again. I did cry the first time I walked across my bedroom."

"Why didn't you tell me?"

"I didn't want you helping me or worrying over me," said Mrs. Robins, patting Melody's knee. She smiled. "Besides, I wanted to surprise you."

"You sure did."

"Before long I'll be doing all my own work," continued Mrs. Robins.

"That's good," said Betty with a loud sigh.

Melody and Mrs. Robins laughed.

"Aunt Lucy will be coming with the girls before long," said Melody. "I think everything's done. I made cookies for them to snack on."

"And there's milk, iced tea, or orange juice for them to drink," added Betty.

"If the rest of the house looks as good as this, you should be very proud girls," said Mrs. Robins, smiling from one to the other. "You did a beautiful job."

"It's all clean," said Melody. "We've been working all day on it."

"Boy, have we!" exclaimed Betty, plopping down on the couch.

"I don't see how you ever did all you do," said Melody. "It was really hard to be the mother for the summer."

"You did a marvelous job, Melody. Didn't she, Betty?"

Betty shrugged. "Most of the time."

"Thanks," said Melody, making a face at her sister.

Just then Matt came in with Randy on his shoulders. "Here's Randy. Clean and ready for his mamma. I gave him a bath and put clean clothes on him." Matt sat on the couch beside Betty and put Randy on the carpet. "I'm going to miss that little fellow."

"He'll miss you too," said Mrs. Robins. "You've been good for him. And for us."

Betty tipped her face up, looking at Matt, and frowned. "You look different, Matt."

"How?" he asked, smiling at her.

Melody looked from one to the other. This was the first time they'd said anything to each other and remained polite.

"I don't know exactly. I mean, you're so good looking. You weren't this good looking before."

Everyone laughed, including Betty.

"Maybe you're seeing my new heart," said Matt, taking Betty's hand. "It shows all over me."

"Maybe that's it," she said, looking down at Matt's hand holding hers, then up into his face. Finally she smiled. The battle between them was over.

Melody looked at her mother and smiled. It made her heart sing to see Matt, the new Matt.

"I'm going to Peru next week," said Matt, looking at Melody. "My folks want me to come help them. They said I could skip a year of college to be with them. It wasn't hard at all to tell them how sorry I am for being such a brat. They said they'd already forgotten."

"I'm so glad for you, Matt," said Melody softly. Her heart almost burst with happiness. She knew how badly Matt wanted to be with his family.

"They're starting a reach-out program for kids. I'll be in charge of that," said Matt.

"That's wonderful," said Mrs. Robins. "You'll do a terrific job. You're so good with children."

"You know, Matt, you won't have to wonder about your future anymore. Your parents will keep you so busy that your future will be planned for you." Melody sat down beside him, twisting so she could look at him.

"I'll love helping them," he said.

"I know you will. I'm glad you came here this summer," said Melody.

"Me too, now," added Betty.

"Any time you want to come stay with us, Matt, feel free," said Mrs. Robins. "I count you as my second son."

"Thank you," said Matt, choked with emotion.

Randy toddled across the floor and stood by the telephone table. "Ho," he said. "Ho."

Betty rushed to him. "He's trying to say 'hello.'" She scooped him up and tossed him high. "Sweety baby Randy."

Just then the doorbell rang.

Help me, Lord, Melody prayed silently.

"It's Aunt Lucy," whispered Betty. "Let me answer. When I open the door, we'll let Randy walk to her."

The doorbell rang again.

Melody waited breathlessly. To her surprise, instead of being upset about Aunt Lucy being there, she was excited because Aunt Lucy would see Randy walking.

"Hurry, Betty," said Mrs. Robins.

Betty dashed to the hall with Randy. She stood him in the doorway of the living room while she opened the door. Randy toddled across to the open door.

"Randy! Baby! You can walk!" exclaimed Lucy, dropping to her knees and hugging the baby. She looked up at everyone with tears in her eyes. "He's so big! I didn't think he'd be so big. And he can walk! How I missed you, Randy." She stood up with him in her arms. "Won't your daddy be surprised."

The trio stood waiting in the doorway, their arms loaded with boxes.

Melody rushed to them. "Girls, come in. It's so good to see you." To her surprise it *was* good to see them. She hadn't realized how much she missed them. "Tell me everything. I want to hear about your trip from the minute you got in the car until you got out again here."

"It'll take us a month to tell you everything," said Jan, laughing.

"Who cares," said Melody, hugging her. "We have plenty of time."

"Put your things on the floor by the couch," said Mrs. Robins.

Melody saw the girls looking at Matt.

"Jan, Sue, Bev, meet Matthew Chamberlain," said Melody cheerfully. "He's a missionary kid. His parents are in Peru and he's going next week."

"That sounds marvelous," said Sue, sinking down beside Matt. "We want to hear all about Peru."

"But first we want to hear about your trip to Mexico," said Matt, making room for the other girls.

"We brought just everything," said Lucy, dropping into a chair with Randy on her lap. She kissed him on top of his fuzzy head. "He's getting hair! He's really getting hair. Oh, Randy!" She kissed him again.

"We've had a good time with Randy," said Mrs. Robins. "He and Matt became the best of friends."

"I'm dying to hear about the trip," said Melody. She was really surprised at herself. She actually wanted to hear. She wanted to see the slides and even listen to any new song the girls worked up. Somewhere along the way the Lord had taken away all the bitterness.

"First let me show you the serape we brought you,"

said Aunt Lucy, reaching for a large package. "Open it now."

Melody pulled off the string that was around the box then lifted the lid. She took out the serape and held it up with a gasp of pleasure. The bright blues, reds, and white made a beautiful design. Melody wrapped it around herself and threw it over her shoulder. "How do I look?"

"Put on this hat and you'll look like a blond Mexican," said Sue, giggling.

"We got you a piñata, Betty," said Aunt Lucy, handing her a large box. "It's in the shape of an elephant. The boys and girls love to hit them and break them open. There is candy inside and it falls to the ground and they make a mad dash to pick it up."

Betty lifted it out by the wire and dangled it in front of her mother. "It's beautiful," she said. "Thanks, Aunt Lucy."

They had a handbag for Mrs. Robins and other things for Mr. Robins and Dave.

"I have the slides in order according to our trip," said Aunt Lucy, handing Randy to Matt so she could get set up.

Jan put up the screen while Lucy put the projector on the coffee table and pulled it back into the right spot.

Melody clicked off the lights and took a seat beside her mother.

"This first batch is us getting started. You can see how full the station wagon was. And this is us crossing into Mexico. We each had to tell our place of birth and were asked if we had anything to declare. They looked through our equipment thoroughly. I don't know what they expected to find but finally they let us pass." Lucy chuckled. "This picture was taken by Jan while I was taking a siesta. She was well repaid later when I took one of her brushing her teeth."

"You didn't put that in, did you?" wailed Jan.

"Of course I did. I'm still repaying you for taking that terrible picture of me."

Everyone laughed, including Melody. She was really enjoying everything that was being said and she loved the slides. She folded her hands in her lap and smiled contentedly.

Aunt Lucy showed slide after slide. Finally she stopped one. "Here is the priest I told you about, Melody. Doesn't he look happy?" She retold the story as she showed different pictures taken in that particular village.

Melody wiped the tears from her eyes, thinking it was a beautiful story.

From time to time the girls added some to the telling. Sometimes Betty or Matt asked questions.

"Altogether it was a trip none of us will ever forget," said Aunt Lucy as Melody flipped on the lights.

"But it is good to be home," said Bev. "I don't think any of us slept well the whole time. And the mosquitoes! Wow. It is good to be home."

"We did get very tired," admitted Lucy, leaning back against the chair once more with Randy on her lap. "But it was worth it. None of us would have stayed home."

There was an embarrassed silence.

"It wasn't as bad staying home as I thought it would

be," said Melody. She was surprised at herself for being able to say it out loud to them. "I did a lot of things this summer that I wouldn't have done if it wouldn't have been for missing the trip."

"She was a great help to me," said Mrs. Robins, squeezing Melody's hand.

"And to me," said Aunt Lucy. "Thanks for taking Randy."

"I can't be left out of the praise corner," said Matt with a grin. "If it hadn't been for Melody of love I wouldn't have become a Christian."

"Melody of love?" asked Jan, lifting her eyebrows. "Melody of *love?*"

Everyone laughed.

"That's a silly nickname that Matt hooked onto me," said Melody, laughing too. "It really didn't fit."

"You can say that again," said Betty.

When the laughter died down, Melody stood up. "We have cookies in the kitchen. Let's go sit around the table where we can be comfortable and eat and talk some more. I can't get enough of hearing about Mexico."

"Did you tell her about that tarantula that almost bit you?" asked Bev, looking at Lucy.

"Did I?" asked Lucy with a shudder.

"No. What happened?"

"It was right after an evening performance. I was just ready to step off the platform when a big hairy spider landed on my foot."

"What'd you do?" asked Betty, holding the pitcher of orange juice.

"I screamed and kicked. That thing flew across the

church and landed with a plop right in front of the pastor. He killed it and got rid of it."

"We tried to get her to repeat that grand performance, but she wouldn't," said Jan, grinning at Lucy.

"She has great lung power," said Sue with a straight face.

Melody enjoyed every bit of the teasing. She was so surprised at herself that at times all she could do was sit quietly and enjoy the lack of the bitterness that she'd had for the summer.

The Lord really did something for me, she thought happily.

"If you'll show me where Randy's things are, we'll be going," said Aunt Lucy, pushing away from the table. "Are you girls ready?"

"Yes," said Bev. "Thanks for the kind attention, Melody. And thanks for letting me go to Mexico."

"I'm glad you got to go," said Melody.

"I'll get Randy's things," said Matt, rushing upstairs.

"He's neat," said Jan, rolling her eyes. "Too bad he's leaving."

"The summer with him? No wonder you didn't miss going to Mexico," said Sue. "What did Wade have to say about him?"

Just then Wade walked in.

"Did I hear my name being used in vain?" he asked, grinning. "Hi, girls. How's Mexico?"

They all answered at once telling him what a great time they had.

"I'm sorry you missed the slides," said Lucy. "But we're going to show them Sunday night at church.

You can see them then. Of course there are a few that I'll remove."

"It's a good thing," said Jan.

"Too bad I couldn't see the slides tonight then," said Wade. "I'd rather see the real trip."

Matt came in loaded down with Randy's clothes. "Tell me where to put them and I'll put them," he said.

Lucy hurried ahead of him to the door. "I'll show you," she said.

The girls said their goodnights and followed them to the car.

By the time Lucy had made a dozen trips back into the house to get something they'd forgotten or tell Mrs. Robins something, they decided it was past time to go home.

"Thanks again, Melody," said Aunt Lucy from inside the car. "See you Sunday."

"Bye. Bye, girls," said Melody. She had her hand in Wade's, and she smiled up at him as the car drove out of the circle drive.

"Let's go for a walk," he said softly.

"Let's. I have time. It's great to say that. I have time, Wade."

"Let's you and I go in and have another cookie," said Matt, catching Betty's hand and pulling her into the house.

"I get the last of the orange juice," said Betty before the door slammed behind them.

Melody and Wade walked hand in hand along the path toward the barn. They looked in on Misty before they walked back toward the house and into the back yard.

"You're very quiet, Melody," said Wade.

"I'm still in shock."

"Did they upset you that much?"

"No. They didn't upset me at all. That's the surprise. I was prepared to have a lousy evening. Instead I loved every minute of it. I've grown in the Lord."

They sat down on the large swing and slowly pushed it back and forth.

"The Bible school accepted me. I leave in ten days."

"Oh." She swallowed hard, fighting tears back. Her heart skipped a beat. "I'll—I'll miss you." She tightened her hold on his hand. "Oh, Wade! I don't want you to go. I can't stand to be apart from you."

"It'll be hard on me too. But, I will be home as often as possible and I'll write every day."

They sat quietly with their fingers locked together, the swing swaying back and forth in a gentle rhythm.

"Will you forget about me after you see all the girls at Bible school?" she asked, her voice just above a whisper.

"How could I forget my Melody of love?" he asked softly as he tipped her chin up and looked into her eyes. "I love you."

"I love you, Wade." She slid her arms around his neck as he kissed her.